Wild

Adrian

ADRIANA

FRENCH

HOT A.F. ROMANCE

AN ALPHA MAN, OPPOSITES *Attract, Billionaire Cowboy*
Romance

I had no idea who that cowboy was, *I swear.*

How was I supposed to know that gorgeous man was billionaire Blade Parker? We were in an airport bar in the middle of nowhere for crying out loud...

I didn't even know I *liked* cowboys until he locked those crystal blue eyes on me from under his

Stetson.

Last night was the first and *only* time I ever—got in the saddle with a stranger. I don't know what came over me. Well, actually I do.

Oops.

Lord help me. If I'd known he was a client there is NO WAY last night would've happened.

Now I have to work with the Parkers on one of the biggest land deals in Montana history.

I'm the only attorney in my office who specializes in real estate.

I'm staying on the Parker's ranch in a trailer parked *right* next to his.

I Can. Not. get sidetracked, no matter how hot af he is.

My career is on the line.

Surely, we can keep things professional, can't we?

SADDLE UP, SUGAR. A new breed of cowboy-cavemen is here. They're dirty and filthy rich. Blade Parker is an alpha male to the nth degree and the first Parker brother to meet in the Billionaire Cowboys Gone Wild Series. Expect humor, coarse language, graphic and steamy situations, and insta-love.

No cheating and a Happily ever after.

Chapter One

UGH ... I RUB MY TEMPLE. My head feels like it's been split down the middle with a dull axe. I grab my giant water bottle and start guzzling, but I know downing all this liquid at this point is futile. Nothing is going to get rid of this hangover. I turn the wheel of my rental into a bend.

Last night was worth it. I grin remembering my cowboy. Okay, he's not technically mine, but my God, was he hot.

I still can't believe I was brave enough to do what I did with him—a total stranger. I've never had a one-night stand before. It's the most shocking thing I've ever done in my whole twenty-nine-year-old life. I don't know if it was my ex's wedding or the fact that I'm almost thirty and alone that pushed me out of my comfort zone or what.

I stopped counting the number of drinks I had at three, two more than usual. And whiskey? I decided to go on a bender with whiskey? Count that as another first. I'm a strictly white wine type of gal.

Let's face it, I was hell-bent on being wild last night—one hundred percent committed to letting loose and pretending I was someone else. Someone slutty else. I should have a big scarlet S for "slut" on my back.

At least there isn't any traffic on these back roads. There's diddly-squat to look at, unless you have a thing for cows. I try to force myself not to think of that nameless sex god, but how can I not? My life is all work. I can't remember the last time I went out and let my hair down with friends.

I think the stranger I met last night might be the best thing to ever happen to me. After checking in at the hotel at Missoula International, my plan was to stay in, take a bubble bath and read the romance novel I picked up at the gift shop. But I'm always alone on these business trips. It gets boring being cooped up by yourself staring at walls, so I got my nerve up and went to the busy hotel bar ... alone. I guess there's a first time for everything—

I ease on the brakes and slow down. Is that a goat standing in the middle of the road? What the heck? I scan the fields and see a small herd on the left. I guess he's trying to catch up with them. It would help if he moved his feet. I blow out a frustrated breath, and even that slight movement hurts my head.

"Anytime, goat. Whenever you're ready." He turns and gives me the eye, like he's deciding whether to move and let me pass or leave me hanging here. I tap the horn. "C'mon, go eat some grass." He slowly drags his butt and crosses the road, making room for me to get around him. "'Bout time," I mutter under my breath. "Say hi to your friends for me."

I shift in the seat and adjust my grip on the wheel. I'm still a little sore from last night. And of course my brain goes right back to him, the most beautiful man I've ever seen. He was well over six feet tall, with huge, corded arms and a big brawny chest that didn't quit. Even his hair was perfect. Once he took off his cowboy hat and stepped out of the shadows toward the bar, my heart went into a conniption. Talk about big dick energy.

When I saw that thick brown hair and chiseled jaw, I started salivating. And the second he locked his eyes on me from across the room and flashed that killer smile, I knew I was a goner.

There were so many women drooling over him. I still can't believe he slid into that empty chair beside me. "What brings you to town, darlin'?" His deep sexy drawl drew me right in, like a bee to honey. Two drinks after staring into his crystal-blue eyes and creaming over him, I was in deep trouble.

I'd never met a man so alpha and masculine. I didn't even know I liked cowboys ... but I've never been more attracted to anyone in my life.

I melted the second he wrapped those big, buffed arms around me. And when he kissed me on that dance floor—and when we practically ripped each other's clothes off and stumbled into the hall, and then the bathroom stall.

Yeah. The bathroom was my idea. Who the hell am I? And where did the old, second-guess, analyze-every-little-thing me go?

That cowboy made my body sing notes I've never been close to touching before. Honestly, his cock was like a massive magic wand. He knew exactly what I needed, when I needed it, and how hard—and, I admit, rough—I wanted him to be.

It wasn't as if I had any desire to be tied up or anything. It had just been so damned pathetically long since anyone had looked at me like a woman instead of an attorney to argue with. I wanted to know what it felt like to be desired ... wildly and wantonly desired.

I got my wish when he slammed me up against the bathroom door—all that and then some. I never knew that kind of intimacy could happen between strangers.

He left his number next to my pillow this morning, but I didn't bring it with me. Why torture myself when I know I'll never see him again? After this job is over, I doubt I'll ever come back to Montana.

I sigh, trying to clear my head. I have to bring my A game to this meeting.

But gawd. I'm still wet for him.

It's like he woke up some secret sex ninja who's been sleeping inside me all this time.

I double-check my GPS and drive up and down the same stretch of empty freeway three times before I finally pull off onto a bumpy unmarked dirt road. Beige dust floats up from the ground and covers my windshield as I slow, leaning over my steering wheel, searching for a place to park.

There isn't any trace of a corporate headquarters; there isn't even a proper building, just a few ramshackle trailers. I turn the car off, grab my phone and get out on shaky legs. They're still like rubber from last night. The sound of the door shutting behind me echoes over the yellow fields.

This can't be right. I press my assistant's number and wait for her to pick up as the blazing sun beats down on my throbbing head.

"Everything okay?" Vivian asks cheerily.

"Whew, I'm so glad you answered. I thought maybe you were on a break."

"Nope. I'm here in the office. What's up?" For the zillionth time since I hired Vivian, I thank my lucky stars I have her on my side. We worked for the same group for years before I had the chance to snag her.

I make a full turn, scanning the desolate landscape. "I think I'm lost. There isn't anyone here."

"Did I get the address wrong?" Vivian asks with a frantic tinge to her voice, and I hear her shuffling through papers. "There was only one address ..."

"I'm sure you did everything correctly. I saw the Welcome to West Palomino sign, so I know I'm in the right town." I clutch the phone to my ear and stare straight ahead at the mountains in the distance. "Could you please double-check the last email Parker Brother Enterprises sent? I'd do it myself, but I'm afraid I'll lose my connection if I move this phone a fraction of an inch."

"You got it. Hold on. I need to jump over to the other computer."

"Thanks." I rub my temple, trying to soothe the pain as I listen to Vivian's heels click and clack across our New York office's marble floors. I lean against the hood of my rental. This is the first time my boss, James Joseph Jr., has sent me out on a job. And this is a big one. I'm the only attorney in our office who specializes in easement disputes.

My pulse starts to race in panic. I can't be late for this meeting.

The Parker brothers just signed the deal on one hundred and sixty thousand acres of prime Montana real estate. They're one of the top ten richest landowners in the state. We all know what the Parkers did in Texas with their successful cattle company, luxury dude ranch, restaurants, and real estate developments, and James Joseph Financial is hoping for a repeat return on investment.

Damn. I wanted to make a good impression, and I'll probably be late. I still have time to make the meeting, but only if it's close by.

"Did you happen to pass a sign that said Flying Hearts Ranch?" Vivian asks. I hear her fingers flying over her keyboard.

"I did. That was the last thing I saw before I pulled up the drive and ended up here. But I'm telling you there's nothing around that even resembles civilization. I saw all the construction and the sign for their housing development, about five miles up the road, but other than that, nothing."

"Are you sure?"

I nod. "All I see is a row of trailers and run-down temporary buildings." I zero in on a barn in the distance. "There might be a horse around here."

"Hmm," Vivian mutters. I picture her at her desk in front of the Manhattan skyline, pursing her lips and frowning. She always does that when she says "hmm." "Well, you're in the right place, as far as I can tell. I've gone over everything. You're technically on the ranch."

"Oh boy ..." I let out a beleaguered sigh. My first big assignment, and I've already blown it. "Shoot."

"Do you want me to call Mr. James's office and check with them?"

"No. Let's not do that." No sense alerting everyone to my mistake. "But stay on the phone with me, okay?" I don't tell her it's because I've suddenly turned into a scaredy-cat.

For a city girl like me, there's something creepy about being lost in a place where no one can hear you scream. I blush as the memory rushes back. It was far more fun screaming "harder, harder" last night. God, his tongue was nothing short of miraculous ...

I shake off the memory before I do something idiotic and start blabbing about my one-night stand to Vivian. She knows me so well, she'd be appalled at my behavior.

The sun glints off the trailers as the massive blue sky envelopes me. The scale of the sky in Montana is mind-blowing. I lean back and stare straight up, trying to wrap my mind around the games my eyes are playing. "I wish you could see this."

"The row of trailers?"

"No. The sky. It really *is* big." I chuckle. "Without any point of reference, high-rises or rolling hills, the sky seems to go on and on. It must be an optical illusion."

"Sounds pretty, if you weren't lost. Hey, I'm pulling up Google Maps again. You've got to be close."

A cool breeze tickles my cheek as I walk past a dilapidated trailer. No signs. No open doors. No nothing. I teeter further down the path in my heels and freeze when I sink into something soft. *Shit.* I look down at my foot. Is it cow poop? Horse?

I make a full turn, looking for wildlife out in the pasture on my left. There could be something hiding behind one of those boulders.

"Hey, do you know if there are any bears around here? I just stepped in ..." I shake my foot and manage to get a clump off. "Whatever it is, it isn't good."

"Chances are there aren't any bears around. I think they're mostly out in the forest. But maybe you should go back to where you saw that housing development before it gets dark. Maybe someone there can help."

"I doubt it. My bet is there's nothing but toothless wonders and men who spend far too much time with farm animals over there." I hear her giggle on the other end.

"Toothless wonder at your service, ma'am." A booming male voice cuts through the still air from behind me.

"Hang on," I whisper to Vivian as a gust of get-the-hell-out-of-here rushes up my spine. I freeze, not knowing where to go. My car is behind me. The voice is behind me, most likely between me and the car.

"What's wrong?" Vivian asks anxiously.

"Remember, if anything happens, check my phone's GPS." I gulp and cautiously turn around.

And gasp.

What. The. Fuck.

My knees buckle and my hand goes to my heart as I take in the dusty, drop-dead gorgeous man. Holy shit. I didn't recognize his voice. Maybe because of all the noise in the bar, or because I was three sheets to the wind, but it's *him*—the cowboy from last night.

I can't even form a word. He's wearing a blue plaid shirt, thigh-hugging jeans, and a smirk wider than the big sky. And oh yeah, he definitely has teeth. Blinding white teeth covered by the full lips I couldn't stop kissing last night. His mouth curves up in a devilish smile. My eyes rake over the broad shoulders I clung to while we were fucking against the wall. I licked that chest about twelve hours ago.

Help me, Jesus.

"Wha—" Under the brim of his Stetson, his stunned blue eyes hit me like a beam of lightning, making the ground beneath me shake. I can't breathe.

"What is it?" my assistant asks. "Everything okay?"

"Listen, I have to call you back." I click the phone off and straighten, trying to get my bearings as my hot-as-fuck fling takes a few long strides in his big boots, closing the distance between us.

"I knew I'd see you again." He licks his chops, making no attempt to hide the fact that he's staring straight at my tits. My nipples instantly go hard and rub against the inside of my bra. Thank

God I still have my jacket on. His stare drops to my legs and slowly roams back up to my eyes. "Did you follow me here, darlin'?"

"What?" I smooth my skirt, kicking the remainder of the poop off my shoe. "No. Of course not," I huff, trying to stay professional when all I want to do is kiss him again. "I'm not a stalker, if that's what you're worried about," I add under my breath, and then remind myself to pull it together. Whatever the hell is going on here could have something to do with the multi-million-dollar business deal I'm working on.

His chiseled face pales. "Don't get me wrong, I haven't been able to stop thinking about that sweet, tight pussy of yours riding my cock last night."

Okay, we're cutting right to the chase here, are we?

"I-I—" For a second, I'm back in the bar with him, ready to latch my thighs around his neck. I swallow thickly and drag my eyes up from the lips that sucked every one of my nooks and crannies to his eyes, trying not to think about the way I came on his tongue, like, fifty times last night … Oh my God. How the hell am I supposed to handle this?

My pulse thuds in my ears. My head is about to spontaneously combust.

I try again, focusing on being calm, cool and collected instead of making an ass of myself in front of the not-toothless-wonder best fuck of my life. "I'm Annalisa Breckenridge." I choke out the words. "From the Joseph James Financial Group."

Chapter Two

SO IT'S *Annalisa* ...

Knowing her name only makes this more real. I thought she was a fucking dream. I step back before I do something crazy like pick up exactly where we left off. Hell, I'd spread her out right here in the dirt if she wanted me to. My chest tightens and my balls swell with the thought. *Man, does she like to fuck.*

When my parents asked me to be part of the welcoming committee for someone from the Joseph James Financial Group, I was expecting the little old lady with horn-rimmed glasses we worked with in Texas.

I can still smell Annalisa on my clothes. I've been as hard as a fence post all day thinking about the way she moaned when she rode my dick till sunrise.

Shit. She's here. It's taking me way too long to process this. My aching head is still in a fog from all the booze last night. I think she made me spank her—

"Welcome!" My mom and dad rush down the path before I have a chance to say a word. "I'm Loretta, and this is my husband, Huck." Annalisa gains her composure and greets them.

No. My brain definitely isn't working right. I'm having a hard time wrapping my head around seeing her with my family.

What the fucking hell?

WILD FOR HER 13

The one time I have a one-night stand, after being abstinent for over a year, it comes around to bite me—just like she nibbled on my ass cheek last night.

And goddamn, is she a smoke show. She's even more stunning in broad daylight, and the way that little business skirt is hugging that sexy ass of hers is killing me. I could fuck her for twenty-four hours straight and never get my fill. I've never had sex with anyone the way we did last night.

"This is our base camp," my mom explains. "The new Airstreams are right over there." She points up the path. "I hope you'll be comfortable."

"I'm sure I will be." Annalisa puts on a stilted smile and cautiously peeks behind my parents, trying to check out her accommodations.

Her long silky brown hair was loose around her shoulders last night. She has it all up in a bun now, obviously trying to play down her looks, but it isn't working. No, it for damn sure is not.

I clear my throat, forcing myself to look away from the tiny waist I gripped when her tight cunt was milking me dry. But it's no use trying to ignore her. The second I plunged into her, I knew she had the power to turn me into an addict.

My eyes rake over her breasts, hidden under her jacket. I had those nipples in my mouth. Those long, smooth legs were wrapped around my hips. Who is this goddess, and where has she been all my life?

"You've met Blade?" My mom sends me a pleasant smile.

"Blade?" Annalisa looks like she's about to pass out.

I'm not about to explain a damn thing about last night's fuck-fest to my parents, and I'm sure Annalisa doesn't want to get into the story of how we met either. "Blade Parker." I extend my big calloused hand and wrap it around hers. Her soft velvet skin melts into mine. My cock shouts against my zipper. *I've missed you!*

"Blade *Parker*?" Her big brown eyes are about to pop out of that pretty little head of hers.

"Yes." Mom smiles obliviously. "Blade's our eldest son."

Annalisa's jaw hits the floor, but she quickly recovers. "Nice to, ahh ... to meet you ... officially," she mumbles under her breath. Her lips quiver while she takes me in like I'm some kind of mirage.

"Shall we get started?" my father asks.

"The office is over here." I lead the way to the trailer we're using temporarily. I don't hear footsteps behind me, so I check over my shoulder. "You coming?"

"Oh, right." She responds like I just woke her up from a nap, and I don't blame her. We didn't sleep more than a few hours last night. "There's an office out here?" She scampers on sky-high heels to catch up with me.

"Yeah. We even have chairs," I tease. "And I could probably get you an appointment with my dentist if you wanted one."

"Oh jeez. You heard that? I'm so sorry, I didn't mean ..."

"To insult one of your biggest clients?" I whisper, so my parents can't hear. I have to admit, I'm enjoying the way she's blushing five shades of pink. Her big brown eyes latch on to mine, and the only thing I see is quicksand. If I get trapped in that danger zone, I'll go straight under, drag her into a trailer and fuck her brains out. Lord have mercy, she should have yellow caution tape wrapped around those curves.

She rushes beside me while my parents trail behind. "I'm sorry. I'm just so surprised to see you here. I'm not used to—I've never done that before—"

My heart cracks a little at how frazzled she is. She's obviously in way over her head and worried. But she shouldn't be. "Forget it."

"Would you?" she asks breathlessly, her voice rising with hope. I meet her gaze, careful not to look for too long.

"I can promise you I won't be forgetting last night any time soon, if ever." I grin when sparks light up her eyes. "But don't worry, your dirty little secret is safe with me."

The corner of her mouth turns up in a sexy half-smile and that's all it takes for my cock to remember the way her pillowy lips were wrapped around it, sucking all the way to the base.

"After you," I say when we reach the trailer.

"Thanks," she says softly, brushing past me, leaving a trace of oranges and jasmine. I can't resist admiring her curvy backside as it sways while she climbs the steps. I rest my hand on the small of her back to guide her up. My cock jumps the second my hand touches her.

I check behind me and see my parents are right on our tail. There's no time to start reminiscing about last night, and I don't want my dream girl to feel like she's being put on the spot, so I force myself to focus on the business at hand.

Annalisa glances around the dingy space, and I point to a chair in front of the desk. "Have a seat."

"Thanks." She avoids my eyes, watching my parents enter the room.

We knew the trailer was a dump the second we bought Flying Hearts Ranch from the Johnsons. This is the first time we've used it—never had any reason to until now. We're using one of the specs as a sales office over at the housing development, but there isn't any place to have a meeting around here besides this trailer.

We pretty much took over the premises as soon as the Feds cleared the place out. Turns out the previous owners were selling drugs over state lines and were only using the ranch as a cover. The pot fields are all burned now.

They found hundreds of kilos of cocaine and heroin stored in hay bales in one of the climate-controlled barns. I have no idea how the Johnsons thought they could get away with such a massive operation. It rivaled some of the larger cartels. They're all in prison now.

I take a seat behind the desk, and my parents sit on either side of Annalisa.

"Please excuse the place, dear." Mom pats her hand. "We're putting all our resources into the new neighborhood."

"Please don't apologize, I completely understand. In fact, I saw the Wild Cat Ridge sign when I drove in."

"We have our first family moving in at the end of the week. We'll be relocating there ourselves as soon as possible." Mom turns, eyes sparkling at Dad.

"Yes," Dad comments without taking his eyes off her. "We'll probably donate these old trailers."

Most people have the wrong idea about my family. When they think of Parker Brother Enterprises, they assume we're all a bunch of spoiled billionaires, living the high life. It couldn't be further from the truth. We've all worked our asses off from day one and sure as shit weren't born with silver spoons in our mouths.

"Please, don't worry about anything on my account." Annalisa primly folds her hands in her lap and straightens with a professional air. She's too young to have been in this business for very long, though she's putting up a good front. "So you're in charge of the whole development?" Her pretty eyes land on me.

"I'm in charge of the Parker Brothers Cattle Company. Everything that happens here at Flying Hearts Ranch is under my jurisdiction."

"We're not wasting time getting up and running. It's all hands on deck," my father explains. "As you probably already know, we have seven children."

"And everyone is in the family business?"

"Correct," Dad answers. "Although they haven't all relocated from Texas yet. Houston and Scarlett are still there."

Annalisa nods. "And you'll have a restaurant and bar too?"

"My brother Cash is running Wild Cat Bar and Grill," I interrupt, bringing her attention back where it belongs, on me. "Essentially, we're recreating what we've already done in Texas. The cattle we raise here will be sold at our restaurants and distributed to others around the country. We'll break ground on Wild Cat Ridge Lodge and Dude Ranch soon."

"And you'll all be part of this community?"

"That's the plan." My mom grins. "Obviously, we're keeping our properties in Texas, but we'll live here too, just outside of the Wild Cat Ridge neighborhood." She reaches over and gives Annalisa's arm a little squeeze, as if they've been friends for years. "We'll have to have you up to the house before you leave. The bedrooms aren't even drywalled yet, but the contractor just finished installing the appliances in the kitchen. And the living room is ready."

Annalisa smiles pleasantly. It isn't a real smile though. I can tell she's still nervous. I'm locked on to the curve of her lips, with an overwhelming desire to make her smile for real. And then I'd kiss her, trail my lips down the curve of her neck, take one of her nipples between my lips—and make her moan.

"As you know, we at Joseph James Financial are here to assist you in your new operation in any way we can." Annalisa leans in. "If you'd like, you can consider me your personal assistant."

"I can think of a thousand ways you could personally assist me, darlin', but none of it has anything to do with the cattle business."

She's temporarily stunned. My mom and dad swivel their necks at lightning speed to pointedly glare at me.

Fuck. I grab the nearest stack of papers and start shuffling. Did I just say that out loud?

My mom glowers.

"No." Annalisa shrugs. "He's right." She gives me a shy smile, and the light coming through the dusty windows makes her dark eyes glisten. "I don't have any hands-on experience with cattle companies, but I do know how to work with bureaucracy."

"Well, we're lucky to have you." Mom raises her brows at me, a silent warning for me to keep it zipped.

"Thank you." Annalisa purses her lips, going into business mode. "My company sent me because I'm the only in-house attorney who specializes in easement disputes. I know the county Roads Department is already trying to restrict development around the access road that leads to the public snowmobile trails."

I'm impressed she's done her research. "They don't have the right to stop us. That road is on our property and runs right through where my herd grazes. Those blasted machines scare the livestock."

Her perfect cheekbones lift in a smile. She's in her element now. "I agree. Legally, the land is yours, but it won't stop the locals from trying to stall your development. One hundred and sixty thousand acres is a lot of land to manage. We'd be better off making friends with the county."

"We're not here to make enemies." Dad shrugs. "If we cut off those snowmobile trails, we're in for a fight."

"Exactly. Don't get me wrong, if they want to tangle with me in court, I'll win." She leans into my dad, and I'm enchanted. I haven't seen this side of her before. Hell, I didn't even ask her what she did for a living last night. Then again, we didn't do much talking ... "But I'd rather not fight if we don't have to. I'll only be here for a week, but I'm confident I'll be able to smooth things over for you with the county and the Bureau of Land Management, should they get involved."

She's a little lioness in heat, and I'm her fucking lion. All I want to do is take her from behind. Every base desire, everything I shouldn't be thinking, obliterates whatever professional code I have left. Hell, we've already fucked, so every code is out the window with her, except the one where I'm burying my face in her pussy.

"James Joseph Senior and I go way back." My dad kicks back in his chair with a wistful smile. "We went to college together. If he sent you, I have all the confidence in the world." He shifts to me. "Blade runs the cattle ranch, so you'll be working primarily with him."

"With Blade?" Annalisa flinches, almost jumping up from her seat.

"I know this land like the back of my hand," I clarify. Her gaze darts to Dad and then back to me.

My guess is she wants to run, but she's all mine now. She just said she's here for seven full days. Wait till I get my lips all over her silky skin again. She'll never want to leave.

"I'll try to stay out of your hair," Annalisa says softly, apparently coming around to the idea that she's stuck with me. "But if it isn't too much trouble, I'd like to have a look at the trail as soon as possible."

"No problem. I'll be happy to show you everything." I lay it on thick, zeroing in on her. She blinks and shifts uncomfortably. "And of course ..." I send her a sly grin. "I'll be sure to give you *everything* you need."

I'M HAVING A HEART attack here.

My fling was with a Parker brother? My gazillionaire client? A man who can have every woman on the planet at his beck and call with the snap of his fingers? Holy hell.

I'm probably just one of a mile-long line of hook-ups. I sure know how to pick 'em. Blade catches me when I sneak a peek. Damn. He's licking his chops, grinning at me.

My heart pounds so hard I'm sure every cow a mile away can hear it. He's going to give me everything I need? The way Blade dropped his voice just then leaves me with no doubt about what he's really saying.

He wants to fuck me again, and Lord help me, I want him to.

"Then we're all set." Huck startles me when he slaps his knees and rises.

Mrs. Parker mirrors his movements. "We'll let Blade get you settled. I look forward to working with you."

You're not going to leave me here, alone with him, are you? "My pleasure," I say, fighting the urge to tear the hell back to Missoula International before I do something stupid like kiss Blade and flush my career down the toilet. But there's nowhere to hide. I take a shuddery calming breath and watch as Blade swaggers out of the office, all sexy as fuck, and walks his parents outside.

I only get a few seconds of relief before he pokes his head back in the door.

"If you're ready, I'll show you to your trailer." His deep voice smooths over me like a blanket of memories. His touch, his kisses, the way he called out right before he came last night invade every crevice of my brain.

The bright blue sky fills the open door behind him as he heads back out. I scramble to my feet and follow him down the steps from the trailer. I stay close behind his big boots and force myself not to look at his fine ass in those jeans. Then he makes a right and goes straight back to my car as if he's reading my mind.

"Would you rather I go? Maybe we can find someone else for you to work with." Panic singes my voice as it zips across the vacant expanse, several decibels louder than it should. I sound like a paranoid moron.

Blade turns so quickly I skid to a stop. "I'm not letting you out of my sight, darlin'. I thought maybe you had bags in the car."

"Oh," I blurt. Of course, he's just being polite. I'm so shell-shocked and out of my league here it isn't funny. "Thanks." I hurry over and pop open the trunk. "I just have the one bag." I instinctively reach in and grab the handle.

"Allow me." Blade's enormous hand skims over mine, scorching my skin with his slightest touch. I flinch and let go of the bag, stepping back from the car as sparks burn through the veins in my hand.

"You're not nervous about being alone with me, are you?" He gives me a lazy, sly smile under the shade of his brim, before lifting my heavy bag effortlessly and closing the trunk.

"No," I lie while my heart plays ping-pong. "We're both adults here."

"After last night, there's no doubt about that, darlin'." He gives me a shit-eating grin, but I'm not touching that subject with a ten-foot pole.

I keep my face blank. He gives me a double take, trying to goad me and make me react, but no way. I'm not falling for those dangerous eyes and dastardly smile again.

"You're over here." He leads the way down the dusty path. I give him plenty of room as a million thoughts pummel my brain.

I fucked a client.

My heart drops. I'm dead if anyone finds out.

Shoot. I stumble on a rock but thankfully catch myself before falling in these damned heels. Not only is my mind in the gutter, I haven't walked on dirt in a million years. Even in Central Park, I stay on the paths.

We pass several shoddy temporary buildings, and then Blade makes a right to two identical trailers parked side by side.

"They look brand new," I say, cutting the awkward silence. "I didn't notice this area when I drove in."

Blade takes a few more steps and stops.

"You knew, didn't you?" he asks sharply, spinning to face me.

"Knew?"

He purses his lips and gives me an unmoving stare. "Be honest. You knew exactly who I was last night."

What is that supposed to mean? I frown, resenting his accusatory tone. What kind of woman does he think I am? "Do you honestly think I'd sleep"—I lower my voice even though there isn't a soul nearby—"with a client? Of course I didn't know."

"Huh." He smirks.

"I said no. Trust me, if I'd known you were part of this deal, last night wouldn't have happened."

"I highly doubt that." His naughty gaze rakes over me. He's almost too good-looking and he knows it. "You wouldn't have taken no for an answer. Couldn't have avoided you if I tried." He lets out a cocky laugh and lifts the suitcase, pointing with it to the trailer on the left. "You're in that one."

"Hey, did you hear me, cowboy?" Blade swivels back to me. "I had no idea who you were. Believe me, I'm just as freaked out about this as you are."

"I never said I was freaked out. I just want to know who I'm dealing with here." He smiles, and now I have no idea what's running through that filthy brain of his.

I fold my arms. "You're dealing with a highly trained professional who only has the best interests of your family in mind."

"That so?"

I adamantly nod. "Yes. And as far as that other stuff—"

"Other *stuff*?" He licks his lips with amusement.

"You know damn well what I'm referring to. Anyway, don't worry. I can assure you it won't happen again. From here on out, our relationship will be strictly professional."

He grins. "Whatever you say, darlin'." And, fuck. His deep, growly voice makes butterflies swarm inside my belly and lower. "Although you shouldn't make promises you can't keep." He chuckles and opens the door.

I'm speechless. What does he have, X-ray vision? Can he see how wet my panties are through my skirt? Does he know what the mere proximity of him is doing to my body right this second? The nerve.

"Some people have to work for a living, Blade. My job is on the line here. Not everyone spends their time idolizing every Parker on the planet, you know. I just thought you were some hot cowboy coming in from the range for a drink. How the heck would I know who you were?"

"Hot, huh?"

I gasp. "You haven't heard a word I said, have you?"

His impish smile widens to a full-fledged grin. Then his ridiculously seductive stare finds my eyes, but I shrug him off. "Oh, freaking never mind," I huff, hurrying in front of him and into the trailer.

Blade follows me inside the cozy space, taking up all the air and bringing his cashmere-and-expensive-leather scent with him. It hits my nostrils like an aphrodisiac, sending me right back to the first time we really kissed—when I had my tongue down his throat, getting down and dirty in the hall right before we fucked in the bathroom. What have I done?

"Sun's going down. Time to rest up." Blade shrugs, and I quickly avert my gaze to stare down at the floor. Then I can't resist and peek up again. He's so big, it's impossible to see anything else but him. I'm so fucked. "We start our days at four thirty around here."

My eyebrows hit my forehead. "Four thirty?"

"I thought I'd let you sleep in." He smiles, rubbing it in. "I'll have coffee ready by the picnic table. If you need anything, I'm next door." He brushes past me, and the touch of his leg sends a bolt of lightning up my spine.

I'm trying to get a grip, but my mind has been blown to smithereens. I can't help but think that being left here out in a field where no one can hear you scream could go a variety of ways.

Right now, I'm having visions of riding that big magic cock of his into the sunset and screaming my head off in ecstasy.

"Thanks again for the help." I grin nervously, like a buffoon.

"Have a good night." He nods. "Oh, and by the way—"

"Yes?" I hold my breath.

"I like you better with your hair down."

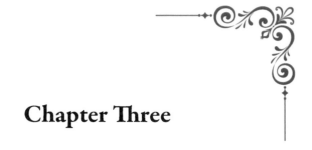

Chapter Three

I HEAD TO MY TRAILER and try to forget how out of place Annalisa looked in the Airstream. Fragile, even. Like she needs me to hold her and protect her. One kiss from me and she'd be putty in my hands, begging me to stay and protect her from wild animals while I ravage her with something far more lethal. I'm hard as a fence post again.

I promised my ranch manager I'd ride out and we'd review the new hands he hired, but I don't feel good about leaving Annalisa by herself. My parents' trailer is a quarter mile up the road.

She could get lost out here. I know she's strong—she has to be, to be as successful as she is—but I like having her in my sight.

I believed her when she said she didn't know who I was last night, but I've been fooled by an innocent act before. My last serious girlfriend had big plans for marriage and even bigger plans for a divorce settlement from me. She was an awfully good actress.

With a name like Parker, my siblings and I have to be careful.

I step up into my Airstream and rub the knots in the back of my neck. The bed in here is better than the one I have back home in Texas. Everything's brand spanking new and top of the line. The television takes up a good portion of the wall, and the sound system rivals the best of them.

She has the same setup next door. I wonder what she's doing.

I try to settle in and polish off a beer. Then I kick back on the bed and see what's on ESPN. There isn't anything of interest, so I check my phone. My family has a text chain and there's usually some kind of drama happening somewhere. I thought I'd hear from Houston, who's still searching for a nanny back in Texas.

All is quiet from my sister, Scarlett, too. She's the youngest, the only girl, and the biggest hellraiser out of all of us. But nothing has blown up since the last time I checked. I toss my cell on the bed beside me and turn the TV on again.

Two hours later, I still can't relax, even after watching the *Great British Baking Show*, which usually does the trick. I like to think of myself as a Renaissance man, and there's something about baking that usually lowers my stress, but not today.

There's just no getting around it. I can't stop thinking about Annalisa. The image of her pussy sliding up and down my cock last night, those big brown eyes, her moans, her kisses, her fucking body—all of it has been seared into my brain with a branding iron.

Fuck. I just remembered she doesn't know where the goddamn picnic table is. She'll be out there stumbling in the dark in the morning. I get out of bed and head out the door.

FOR THE FIRST TIME in my life, I wish I had some kind of drug to relax me. How am I supposed to sleep with Blade so close?

I sigh and check out the space. I knew I'd be on a construction site at some point during this trip, but I wasn't planning to live on one. I thought the Parkers would have a guest house, somewhere with streets and sidewalks, to put me up in. Just add this to my list of surprises today.

But if you're going to live in a trailer, I guess a new Airstream is the one to be in. It's spacious, with a dining area and kitchen; there's even a little couch. My stomach has been rumbling for the last hour, so I check the fridge and find it packed with drinks and food. Maybe I can get through this ordeal after all.

The bed is ready and waiting, dressed with a fluffy new comforter and crisp white pillows. My poor, weary body is about to call it a day.

My hangover has eased a bit but not much. The second I spotted Blade, my splitting headache came roaring back.

I dig through my luggage and pull out my comfy oversized T-shirt and some shorts to sleep in. Unpacking can wait till the morning. That bed is calling to me.

I get out of my suit and change, feeling immediate relief the second I take off my bra. After locking the trailer door, I grab a water and sandwich from the fridge and take them with me to bed.

Nighttime in New York is probably as loud as it is during the day. When I'm home, the blaring sirens, honking horns and chatter blend into a muffled white noise that lulls me to sleep.

Here, the silence is deafening.

Trying to keep my brain from racing, I tear the Slo Mo wrapper off my sandwich. I drove past the sign on the way in. The place looked abandoned. If I'd known they sold food there, I would've stopped. I chomp into the roast beef and try to acclimate to the nothingness around me.

The more I listen to the quiet, the more unnerved I become.

Ugh. Forget it. I need noise.

I grab the remote and flick on the giant flat-screen. The local news anchors soothe me with their chatter about the weather.

Looks like we have clear days, chilly nights ahead, but mild temperatures for June.

The bed isn't bad. I shift, wedging a pillow behind my back, and take another bite. A knock on my trailer door makes me bolt upright. I quickly swallow and turn down the TV.

Another knock comes.

Is there a change in the schedule tomorrow? Did something come up?

I scramble out of bed and check out the window. It's pitch black out there now, so I can't see a thing, and there's no peephole on the door.

"Who is it?" I ask cautiously.

THE SOUND OF ANNALISA'S voice makes my cock ache.

"Just your friendly neighborhood toothless wonder."

"You're never going to let me live that down, are you?" she says, before the door swings open and I blank.

I think I was going to say no or come up with another wisecrack, but I've got nothing.

She's wearing a skimpy shirt with no bra. Her pebbled nipples and high, firm tits are so perfect, it's like she coldcocked me. Fuck. Her legs go all the way to the stars in those shorts. I have my own porn show standing in front of me.

I'm speechless.

"What's up?" Annalisa parks a hand on her hip and looks down, leaning against the door frame. Then she realizes what has my cock leaking pre-cum and looks down at herself.

"Crap, I'm not dressed." She jumps, looking horrified, and ducks behind the door.

"It's not a problem, darlin'." I lick my lips, grinning. "Nothing I haven't seen before."

"Funny." Annalisa pokes her head around the side of the door. "I wasn't expecting company."

This was a bad idea. I'm salivating now, ready to tear that door off the frame. "I just wanted to make sure you knew where the picnic table was."

"Oh?"

"Yeah." I point down the left side of her trailer. "It's right behind us, kind of hidden by shrubs. But there's a big oak tree with a swing in front of the table. Head for the oak and you can't miss it. Bring your phone in case you need the flashlight."

"Thanks, I will."

"And if you need anything, there are contact numbers on the counter next to the sink. I'll be back probably late in the afternoon." I start for my trailer.

"Wait a minute."

I turn.

"You're going to be gone tomorrow? All day?"

Wow. Progress. She's already missing me.

"It's a regular day at the office for me, but don't worry, maybe we can get together tomorrow night ..."

Her eyes narrow.

"Or tonight, if you'd like ..." My cock bangs at my zipper. *Honey, I'm home!*

She smirks and shakes her head. She steps in front of the door again, so miffed she doesn't realize she's giving me another porn show.

"This isn't about having a sleepover. I told you, it's strictly business between you and me from here on out."

I study her face, and I see she's serious. Hell, she's not going to make it easy for me, is she?

"You said I could come to work with you," she says.

"I did no such thing." I step back, trying to keep my eyes off those Hershey kisses poking through her shirt. "Whatever gave you that idea?"

She blows out a breath and crosses her arms, making her nipples jiggle, which is the equivalent of giving crack to an addict for a breast man like myself. I force myself to focus on her pretty brown eyes.

"When we were in the office with your parents," she explains, "your dad said that you were the one I'd be working with, remember?"

I shrug. "Yes, but having you following my every move tomorrow isn't a good idea. In fact, it's a dangerous one."

She doesn't back off. "I thought you could show me where the snowmobile access road is. I know exactly where the border is on the map, but it would help me finalize my plan if I saw it in person."

She puts up a good argument, I'll give her that. But what do you expect from a lawyer? "I have a lot of work to finish before I can take you on any guided tours. And I can promise you, you won't enjoy any of it."

She shrugs me off. "You might think I'm just a city slicker, but I'm tougher than I look. I can handle being out there all day. I promise I'll stay out of your hair."

"Did you bring boots?"

"Of course. They were the first thing I packed."

I rub my lips and study her suspiciously. "And you know how to ride a horse?"

"Yes," she harrumphs, shaking her head. "Abso-friggin-lutely, cowboy."

I raise my brows and she cracks up, easing the tension between us. And hell, when she smiles at me like that? "Okay. You win. If you're ready and out by the picnic table at four thirty, you can ride with me."

"Perfect." She laughs, smiling from ear to ear. "Thank you! I'll see you there."

She's so adorable that I say, "Good night," before any other crazy idea starts popping out of my mouth.

I get back to my place with my throbbing cock pointing the way. There's no way I can relax now after seeing her half naked.

I take a quick shower, down a double whiskey and get in bed with a massive tent in my shorts.

Fuck. I thought I'd never see her again.

I close my eyes, remembering the first time I laid eyes on her across that crowded room last night. She fucking took my breath away.

The bar was dark, but it was like she had her own light source. Her eyes met mine and pulled the floor out from under me. I've never seen a more beautiful woman in my life.

And when I dragged her onto the dance floor, which was only an excuse to hold her tight, she was a fucking wet dream in high heels.

I tug down my shorts and grip my aching dick. Fuck. Her kisses tasted like whiskey and sugar.

I spread my pre-cum around my fat, throbbing crown and stroke down, reliving every second of last night, just the way it happened.

All breath, she begs me to fuck her, her perfect tits plastered to my chest. She won't give me her name, so she's Sugar-whiskey to me. Her hard nipples could cut glass right through that thin silky blouse of hers. She might be dressed in a business suit, but her body is made for sex. All I want to do is get to her skin and fuck her juicy pussy.

"No, this can't be happening," she chokes out. I slide my hand down her back and grip her fine ass.

"But it is, baby," I growl, pressing my palm on her curvy round bottom, pulling her flush against my aching cock. "This is for you, sweetheart."

I groan as I relax into the mattress, squeezing my balls and stroking my bat from the base all the way to the top and down again.

Sugar-whiskey's eyes flash fire, a smoldering gold mixed with melted chocolate. "I want you to keep your eyes open and watch when I fuck you," I say, inhaling her sultry jasmine-and-orange perfume. I move her blouse's collar with my nose and suck the delicious curve between her neck and shoulder.

"Oh God," she whimpers throatily, arching back, giving me better access. "Here?" She grinds her hot pussy against me. "On the dance floor?"

"Too many questions." I find her mouth and plunge my tongue between her lips, fucking her with my tongue the way I will with my cock.

We're in our own whiskey-buzzed, hazy world as we kiss each other hungrily, like we've been starving all our lives, clinging to each other in a frenzy of tongues and sweat.

There's no way we're going to be able to carry on without one of us coming here on the dance floor. I bring my hand around to her front and slide it up her silky thigh. My cock drips in agony.

"Now," she groans, desperately reaching for my buckle. The sexy cupcake's dying for me to pump her full of cum, and she'll soon get her fill. I'm claiming her tonight, and she'll never want another cock again.

"Now." I walk her backward toward the only dark corner I can find. Fuck, I can't take my lips off her long enough to see anything. We half walk, all the while kissing and feeling each other up.

We stagger, breath on breath, holding each other, and finally reach the dark hall across the bar. My big paws find her luscious breasts, and I knead her tits through her top.

Sugar-whiskey's delicate hand finds my dick. Holy fuck. I close my eyes as my cock threatens to break through the fabric. She's trying to jack me off through my jeans. Two more seconds of that and I'll come in my pants.

In a heartbeat, she latches her hands around my neck and pulls me into a ladies' room I didn't know was there.

Whatever she wants goes.

I stroke faster and harder, keeping my eyes closed. I'm with her now, just like last night. I see her clearly. I can even smell her.

Fuck. I moan as I jack myself off, imagining it's Annalisa. Up and down, up and down ...

She's going to come so hard and be so limp that I'll have to carry her out of this bar. The second we get inside the ladies' room, our mouths crush together. I hold her close, keeping her tight against me, slamming the door shut with my back. Clawing at her buttons, I quickly get that fucking blouse out of my way—

Christ.

My dick pulses and my heart hammers at the sight of her.

She so fucking perfect. Sexier than I imagined. I clasp her creamy round breast with my rough hand and tug her bra down, freeing the raspberry-pink bullets I've been hard for all night. With a grunt, I latch on to a nipple with my mouth and tug.

"Yes." She throws her head back, thrusting her breast against my mouth. Her long brown hair sways over her shoulders as her hands glide down my chest to my belt. She unbuckles it in less than a second and presses her hot lips on mine. Her sweet moans fill the room as we pant between wet, open-mouth kisses and trip into one of the stalls. Sugar-whiskey frantically hikes up her skirt, and I tear her panties off in one swoop.

She's mine.

Fuck me, baby. I spit on my palm so I can feel her slick, wet pussy. I stroke up and down, putting my arm into it, getting myself off faster and harder. I close my eyes as my skin-on-skin sounds fill the trailer.

Sugar-whiskey reaches up and grips the stall door. She finds the toilet seat with one of her high-heeled shoes and braces herself on it, as I spread her legs wide, opening her juicy pussy like a gift.

"Fuck me, cowboy," she begs against my lips. Under hooded lids, her fiery eyes plead with lust. "Fuck me." I pin her to the wall. Gripping her hips, I plunge my throbbing cock up into her. She cries out in pleasure.

I roar at the sound. My heart's about to beat out of my chest. I watch, transfixed by the sight of her small, hot glove expanding around my thick, girthy rod, taking every fucking inch, coating me with her cream.

"Fuck," I growl as her walls clamp around me. I crush her lips with mine, and we find our rhythm, banging each other into a frenzy.

My hand slides up and down my pulsing dick. Up and down, up and down, I rock my hips as I beat myself off, groaning in pleasure. *Fuck my cock, baby ... Just like that.*

"Harder," she begs, riding my dick for all it's worth, taking me with her somewhere up in the clouds.

I can't see straight. My need for her is blinding. I'm obsessed and nothing can tear me away from her. Not ever. "You're mine." I pump up into her like an animal. She'll never forget whose cock she belongs to. Her back's to the flimsy wall that rattles and shakes as we pound against it.

"Come for me," I say, fucking that tight pussy harder. "I'm going to fill you so deep with my cum, I'll have it dripping out of your pretty little mouth. Is that what you want?"

"Yes." Her sweat-coated tits jiggle, spilling from her bra. She hangs on to the door and bounces up and down on my dick, faster and faster. "Oh shit! I'm coming." Her grip tightens around me, milking my thumping cock, and she trembles as the orgasm tears through her. She screams out in ecstasy and lets go of the door to cling to my shoulders with both hands.

The sound of her coming shoots through my veins, turning my blood to molten lava. My heavy balls contract, ready to spill. "Damn." I clench my jaw and hang on, not letting go until her last wave is over.

"Fuck," I choke out. I break loose, coming so hard I lift off the bed as my warm seed spurts all over my stomach. "Fuck." I shake, jerking myself until every drop is gone and I collapse back down on the bed.

Chapter Four

THE HOTEL ELEVATOR door dings closed. His lips crush mine in a frantic kiss. My hands latch around his shoulders as he presses me into the wall. I close my eyes, inhaling leather and cashmere. I don't know what kind of cologne he wears, but it smells expensive, and I'm drowning in luxury. His hard cock throbs with demand against me. The stubble on his cheek scrapes my skin as he groans in my ear, making my pussy drip with need. I want him so badly I'm aching at my core.

Gasping for breath, the cowboy breaks the kiss and meets my eyes. His hands clasp my face and I blink, feeling the electricity spark when his dangerous eyes fix on mine. The heat of his glistening blue stare tells me everything I need to know. He wants me.

Every cell is shouting *fuck me. Fuck me.* I whimper into his mouth. His tongue finds mine and I suck it hungrily, my pussy pleading for this beautiful man.

"You're so fucking sexy," he says against my lips, playing my body like a maestro as he cups my breast. He finds my tender nipple and rolls it between his thumb and index finger. I arch my back needily and wrap my leg around his, grinding on his hard, massive cock.

I can't get enough of this man. His hand strokes my thigh, igniting my skin, then travels slowly, torturously, closer to my bare pussy.

A sly half-smile curves his lips as his hand glides over my skirt and reaches under. His finger finds my slippery wet slit, and I pull in a sharp breath when he presses a finger and then another inside me. I cry out, balancing on one heel, the other still clinging to his thigh. His big hand comes around and grips my bare ass, holding me in place as his fingers curl up and find my G-spot.

"You're so fucking wet," he growls, low and throatily, into my ear. His massive thumb circles my clit as his fingers work my G-spot.

"Fuck." Panting, I find his lips again. How is he doing this? How many fingers does he have? So many sensations are ripping through my system that I'm about to pass out. I grind down on his hand, trembling and shaking, feeling the pressure build. "Fuck." I gasp for a breath. "You're going to make me come again, cowboy."

"And wouldn't that be a shame." His thumb finds my throbbing nub again. "I love watching you come." I rock my hips, fucking his fingers, humping his palm.

"Oh my God." I let out a long, aching moan. The orgasm hits like a tidal wave coming down hard, and I'm swept under, losing my balance. He holds me steady, and I grip his arms and shriek into his shoulder. My pussy clenches around his fingers as I spasm, bucking against him. Shit. I've never come so many times in one night in my life.

His lips crash to mine and I melt, relishing his whiskey taste and expert tongue. "I don't think you should ever wear panties again," he says mischievously.

"If I didn't wear panties, you wouldn't get to rip them off me," I tease back, foggily remembering that we left my underwear in shreds in the bar bathroom. "And where's the fun in that?"

"You know what else is pretty funny?" His deep voice reverberates through my system.

"No, what?"

"I forgot to press the button."

"No." I close my eyes, forgetting my thought as his finger teases over my sensitive clit. "You didn't forget." I tremble. "You've pressed my magic button, what, fifty times tonight?"

"What floor to your room?" he whispers against my lips with a chuckle.

"Oh ..." I finally get what he's asking. "Seven."

The cowboy keeps one strong arm around me and reaches back to the elevator panel. He presses the number and comes right back to my lips.

"Maybe she needs her rest." An unfamiliar woman's voice interrupts us from somewhere far away. I stir under the cozy blankets. "She had a long day of travel yesterday," the woman continues. "No, don't wake her up. Blade, let her sleep."

My eyes blink open as my brain starts processing the conversation. The sleepy fog starts to clear. The hazy dream fades and the words "let her sleep" come into focus. *Sharp* focus.

Crap. "I overslept!" I say the words out loud as if hearing them could make me move faster.

Crap, crap, crap. I pull the covers off and tear out of bed to my still unpacked suitcase. Slamming it down on its side, I rummage through the neatly folded bundles of clothes. Hurriedly, I fling off my sleep clothes and slip into my new Levi's and J. Crew flannel shirt. I might be late, but at least I'll be dressed for the occasion.

I race to the door and stick my head out. "Be right there," I yell. "Sorry!"

"No worries. Meet us at the table."

"Thanks." I shut the door and scramble back to my suitcase. Leaving my warm fuzzy socks on, I shove my feet into my brand-new Ralph Lauren boots. I grab my heavy down coat and stick my cell phone and sunglasses into the pockets.

I rush to the bathroom and quickly brush my teeth. Hell. I glimpse at my scary reflection and wipe the sleep from my eyes and splash water on my face. There's no time to put sunblock on. On the way to the door, I pinch my cheeks to try to get some color on my face.

The sky is just waking up too. It's a soft shade of apricot as I race past the yellow field sparkling with dew toward the oak tree. The mountains look like they've been painted in shades of lavender, from the lightest almost-pink, where the mountains meet the land, all the way up to the summit where they're a dark purple. I was so frazzled yesterday, I hadn't taken the time to notice how magnificent this place is.

"Glad you could make it." Blade's deep voice makes me blush with embarrassment when I reach the picnic area. *I didn't mean to dream about you.* He's wearing one of those cowboy jackets, light brown with a fur collar. His dark brown Stetson matches the jacket perfectly. My pussy pulses with dirty memories. I must've played with myself all night.

"Sorry, I'm late," I guiltily blurt to no one in particular and make my way over to his parents by the grill. *Nice way to make an impression.*

"Morning, Annalisa." Loretta's blonde hair is neatly coiffed. Her blue eyes are bright, as if she's been awake for hours. I make a mental note to be just like her when I'm in my sixties. I didn't realize how pretty she was yesterday. Fit and trim, she's one of those natural beauties at any age. A warm smile covers her face as she clasps my hand. "Did you sleep well?"

"I did, thank you." *If I remember correctly, your son went down on me.* "That bed is so comfortable, and the trailer is just beautiful."

Huck adjusts his horn-rimmed glasses. "Come." He leads the way back to the picnic table, with Loretta by his side. "We saved some breakfast for you."

"Thank you, but you didn't have to do that."

There are dishes on the table, napkins and condiments. The only setting with a fresh fork and napkin is in the spot next to Blade. "Morning." I sheepishly steal a peek at his smooth, freshly shaved, perfect jaw. And those lips—

I slide in next to Blade's hunky body on the bench, careful to keep a professional distance and not brush against him. I don't need to be struck by any of his lightning bolts today.

He pushes back from the table and looks down at my feet. "Those aren't the only boots you brought, are they?"

I meet his eyes, wondering how an intelligent man can miss something so obvious. "They're riding boots, for your information." I place my napkin on my lap and side-eye him. Does he have to look so gorgeous this early, and smell so good it makes me want to lick him?

"Here you go, darlin.'" Loretta hands me a metal cup filled to the rim. The steamy mug warms my hands, and the heavenly smell of caffeine goes right into my veins. "I'll bet this is a lot different than a New York Starbucks." She takes the seat across from me.

"I'll say," I comment before taking my first sip. "Thank you. This is delicious." I savor the rich blend of java. I have no idea what brand of coffee this is, but it's the best I've ever tasted.

"So tell us," Loretta asks, "what do you think of our little slice of paradise?"

"The walk here from my trailer was beautiful, but I haven't seen much, to be honest. Just what was there on the drive in from Missoula." *Oh, and your son's massive penis.* I flush, pushing the thought out of my brain. "It sure is quiet, I'll give you that."

Blade bumps my leg and chuckles beside me.

I hold back a grin, staying perfectly professional. "I'm so used to all the racket in New York, I had to turn on the TV last night so I could fall asleep." I feel Blade's invasive stare bore into my left temple. I quickly turn, catching him in the act.

"What?" I whisper.

"Nothing," he says casually, setting his mug down. "Just wondering how you're going to ride in those boots."

I frown and look under the table at my beautiful new Ralph Laurens. Please. He has nothing to worry about. If anyone knows country, it's Ralph. "I told you, they're specifically made for riding. Trust me. I'm prepared."

"Whatever you say, darlin' ..."

I sigh, focusing my attention back on Loretta. "I was so happy you have Netflix here. I've gotten into the habit of watching the *Great British Baking Show* at bedtime when I'm home."

Blade narrows his eyes at me, before grabbing the carafe and topping off his cup.

What was that look about? "I like the show, is all," I huff. Jeez, I have to explain what I watch on Netflix?

"Blade's been baking since he was a little boy," Huck says from the grill. "Isn't that one of your favorite shows, Blade?"

"You bake?" I nudge him with my elbow.

He gives me a half-smile that shouldn't make my heart skip, but it does. "What can I say? I'm a man of many surprises."

"He used to make the most adorable mud pies, remember that?" Loretta calls out to Huck.

"I've come a long way." Blade grins, and the three of them share a look that makes it impossible for me not to feel the love between them.

I wistfully think of my father. It'll be the two-year anniversary of his death this December, but when he was alive, my dad, mom and I all had our special bond too. He was a lawyer too and encouraged me to go to law school.

I laugh to myself. Come to think of it, I don't think I ever saw my dad out in nature, unless you count him lounging by our pool. We'd take weekend drives to the country sometimes, but his version of country wasn't anything like this.

The caffeine begins to kick in and I thankfully start to perk up. "I can't wait to get a good look at that snowmobile access road. I was thinking last night we might want to approach the county with a compromise."

Loretta nods in response.

"It's never good to talk about business on an empty stomach." Huck sets a heaping plate of eggs, bacon and toast in front of me. "I hope you like it."

"Thank you so much." My mouth waters. "I can't remember the last time I actually sat down for breakfast. It's usually just coffee to go. You're going to spoil me here." Blade eyes me as I take a bite of the buttery scrambled eggs.

I ignore him, deciding to not feel self-conscious despite him watching my every move.

I'm going to enjoy every forkful, because I'm starving. I take my first bite, and it's so good I catch myself moaning out loud. I cover my mouth, trying to take it back, and see Blade smiling at me. I can't help but get lost in his dangerous stare for a few seconds before I pull myself out of fantasy land. "This is delicious. Thanks again."

"You're welcome." Huck points to the grill. "You can cook practically anything out in the fresh air."

I dig in to my plate with gusto. I'm a little concerned I'm keeping everyone waiting, but they don't seem to be uptight about anything.

For a family of billionaires, the Parkers sure don't seem to live it up very much either. You'd think they'd have a personal chef, and a butler, but they seem perfectly happy with the way things are.

Loretta catches my eye. "You were saying something about a compromise?"

"Right." I wipe my mouth with the napkin. "I was thinking about the possibility of cutting in another access road to the public trails. We could build a road on the perimeter, set it back a few miles, or however much you need to protect the herd. That way, the locals could still enjoy being out in nature with their snowmobiles, and the cows can munch their grass in peace."

"I guess building a hospital for the town isn't enough," Blade cracks.

"No, I like this," Huck interrupts. "It's a win-win for everyone. The benefit would far outweigh the cost. Our hope is to add to the West Palomino community, not take anything away. It would be nice to start out with the locals on our side."

I nod, relieved we're on the same page. "Then we should be proactive and make the offer before anyone files any grievances or complaints."

"It sounds like you have a full day then." Huck rises from the table with his plate, and Loretta starts clearing. She refuses my help, so I gulp down the rest of my coffee. I've already inhaled my breakfast.

"I can't wait to see the property." I tilt my head and eye Blade cockily. He checks me out with a suspicious gleam in his eye.

The Parkers don't have those heavy southern accents. I was expecting a lot of "y'alls" and "all y'alls", but they only have the slightest of drawls. But I put on my best twangy accent anyway and give Blade my most charming smile. "Looks like it's time for us lil' doggies to saddle up and get a move on, pardnuh."

Chapter Five

THERE'S NOTHING MORE annoying than someone trying to put on a fake accent; I don't care what kind it is or whose mouth it's coming out of. I give Annalisa my steeliest stare, narrowing in on her eyes without blinking.

She cheekily stares right back, and I hold firm. A look of shock and anxiety takes over her face, and I crack. I can't help it and start laughing. Coming from her, that damn accent is cute. She breaks into a smile as it dawns on her I was only teasing. Everything about Annalisa is fucking cute and sexy at the same time. That's what makes her so damn intoxicating.

"We better clear out, we've got a big day, but could y'all hold back on the lil' doggy references?"

"Deal." She laughs. "Let's do this." She springs up from the bench and I point to the stables about twenty yards away.

"Ready?"

"That's why I have my new boots on," she says, cheerfully hurrying ahead to the horses.

I catch up with her right as she gets to my big bay Merle's stall. I grab a rope off the wall, wrap it around his neck and lead him to where we keep the saddles. I eye one of the stirrups and glance down at her boots.

Annalisa watches intently. She isn't going to be happy about what I have to do next. "I need to check your heels. Let me see them."

"My heels?" She extends her hands, palms up.

"The heel of your boot." I point down.

"Oh, sure." She turns so her back end is facing me, and I squat. Lord have mercy, her sexy ass is inches from my mouth. What I wouldn't do to rip those jeans off and swipe my tongue down her crack to the front. I glance at the stack of hay bales in the corner, my filthy brain shifting gears. If I laid a blanket down on the top bale, the possibilities could be endless.

Annalisa primly lifts her right foot. I force myself to stay on task, which is *not* to eat her pussy in the barn, in broad daylight, with my parents nearby. I swallow, willing my cock to settle down.

I have a feeling I already know what I'm about to see. I take hold of Annalisa's delicate foot, take some liberties, and grip her slender calf too. My pulse hammers as I fight the temptation to glide my hand up her thigh. Those jeans are skintight on her. Her sweet little cunt is so close to my face ... I clear my throat and gently place her foot back on the ground.

"Nope. Sorry. Not gonna work." I get the hell away from her as fast as I can before I lose control, back her into the wall, and fuck her just the way I did in that bathroom stall.

I stroll to the wall and grab Merle's brush off the hook.

"What do you mean it's not going to work?" Annalisa trails me, frowning. "I spent a fortune on these boots. They've got to work, that's what they're made for."

I give Merle a quick brush down and straighten the saddle blanket over his back. "I don't know much about English riding. Maybe they'll work for that. But those boots won't do you any good with a western saddle."

I grab the saddle off the wooden horse and place it on Merle's back. "And in case you haven't noticed, that's how we ride around here. *Western.* Real western sometimes. It can get dicey out there. I can't risk anything happening to you." I turn back to Merle and secure the saddle straps. I don't hear a peep from Annalisa, so I check behind me.

Her lips are pursed; her forehead is wrinkled—that brain of hers is spinning a mile a minute. She looks down at her boots and then the saddle. Crap. I don't like to see her so worried, and I sure as shit hate the fact that she isn't happy.

Having her here is going to be the death of me. I'm never going to get a damn thing done if all I'm trying to do is either fuck her, eat her pussy, or make her smile.

"Look," I say, lifting the left stirrup. "See how big this opening is here?" Annalisa steps beside me, smelling like jasmine and the next good fucking she needs. That'll make her smile—

"I see." She nods.

I point to her feet. "Those heels will slip right through this stirrup. English saddles have smaller metal stirrups. Maybe your heel would be big enough to catch on to an English stirrup before it slid through, but not with this one."

She's listening intently, but her forehead is still scrunched. She's obviously not getting it.

"One wrong move, just the quickest turn, the slightest unexpected jolt, and your foot goes through the stirrup. The horse bolts and you're dragged. There would be nothing I could do to stop it. By the time I got the horse under control, your neck could've snapped, or God knows what else." My stomach churns at the thought of her being dragged. My chest tightens. What the hell would I do if anything like that happened to her? I couldn't bear it.

A heavy ache rakes through my system. I know she's going to put up a fight, but this conversation is over. No way am I letting her on a horse in those flimsy boots. I can't even look at her because she'll think she'll have an opening and start arguing. I knew it the first night in the hotel that her brain works the same way mine does. That's why were so fucking good at fucking.

I put Merle's bridle on and glance back at Annalisa over my shoulder. She hasn't moved an inch and looks disappointed as hell.

"Hey," I say gently. "I appreciate you wanting to see the lay of the land, but I'm sorry. I just can't be responsible for anything bad happening to you."

I take hold of the reins and horn, dig my left foot into the stirrup, swing my right leg over Merle and ease into my saddle.

"So that's it?" She crosses her arms and scowls up at me. She's shooting daggers from her pretty eyes like the wild cat she is. "You're just going to leave me here and prevent me from doing my job?" She makes a full turn, searching for something. Another pair of boots? Feed? Hay? Damned if I know. "Well, can I at least drive there?" she asks hopefully. "To wherever you're going?"

The sun is streaming in through the open barn doors and doing crazy things to her sparkling eyes. They're almost golden in this light. Jesus, every time I see her from a different angle, she takes my fucking breath away again.

I sigh. And then grin as the thought strikes me. I doubt she'll go for it. "There is *one* way for you to join me, but I don't think you'll like it." Because at some point during the ride, I'll most likely come in my pants.

"Try me."

She's not going to take the bait. But hey, you can't blame a guy for trying. "You could ride with me." I scoot back and tap on the saddle front of me. "Right here." I send her a devious smile. "See, you have options, darlin.'"

She frowns, looking me up and down suspiciously. "You mean both of us on the same saddle?"

"That's exactly what I mean." I take hold of the reins and turn Merle, leading him out of the barn. "Better make up your mind. We're burning daylight," I shout over my shoulder but keep the horse at a slow walk, giving her plenty of time to stew. I'm smiling ear to ear. I know the temptation is killing her.

My cock is already bumping against my zipper, making my ride uncomfortable enough. I don't need to have her fine ass rubbing up against me. I guide Merle out through the open gate. "I'll be back after dark," I shout.

"Wait!" Annalisa calls out. "Wait up!"

What the hell? I pull on the reins and bring Merle to a stop. Annalisa takes quick strides toward me. Her mouth is a straight line, her hands clenched in steely determination. "I want to ride with you. I didn't come all the way out here to stare at the inside of a trailer, and I need to write that proposal."

Well, I'll be damned. "You sure about this? Once we get started, there'll be no going back. I won't have time to turn around if you change your mind."

She brings a hand over her eyes to shield them from the sun and looks up at me. "You heard what I said, cowboy. I'm tougher than I look. I can handle getting into the saddle with you. The question is, will you be able to handle me?"

"Ha!" I hold onto the horn and burst into a laugh, a loud, full belly laugh, the first in a long time. "I've handled a lot of women wilder than you in my saddle, darlin'." I lie—there's no one on the planet wilder than her. Not when it comes to fucking, at least. I wink, waiting for her to turn on her English riding heels and head straight back to the trailers.

She doesn't. She juts her chin out and stays put.

I'm surprised. Flat-out shocked, to be honest. It looks like we're actually going to do this. My cock's so happy it's doing a damned two-step against my zipper.

I wave her over. "Suit yourself." *But don't blame me if you feel a rod behind your ass.*

Annalisa hesitates for a second and then approaches. "Okay, now what?"

How 'bout we just blow this ride off and you suck my cock in the barn? My heart hammers as I lock on to her mouth. Oh, how I'd love to slide my big dick through those pillowy pink lips again. Fuck. She couldn't get enough of me. I shake my head, trying to clear the thought from my brain.

It's been a long time since I rode double. I've only done it in an emergency, maybe once or twice when I was younger for pleasure. With my balls about to burst, I carefully climb down from Merle.

"Wh-what are you doing?" Annalisa takes a big step back.

"I'm helping you up. You want to ride or not?"

She releases a sigh and closes the distance between us. I slide my arm around her curvy waist, dig my foot in the stirrup and haul her up with me into the saddle in one swoop before she changes her mind.

Her silky hair tickles my nose. My blood roars with fire at the closeness of her. She's such as sexy-as-fuck little thing. Annalisa scoots forward, trying to put some space between us, but her ass crack is right next to my cock.

Once we start riding, hell, I might as well be humping her. I'm so hard I could ram through a steel wall right now. This is going to be one hell of a ride.

I reach around her and adjust the reins. My arms are locked around her on both sides, keeping her safe. There's no way she'll fall off. My heart pounds, and my chest is tight as I make a clicking sound, giving Merle the cue to start walking.

This is the first time I've been able to get Annalisa in my arms since our night together. She's a damn perfect fit.

Chapter Six

BLADE'S HULKING BODY is behind me. His massive corded arms keep me parked in the saddle. I hold on to the saddle's horn for balance and try to keep myself positioned at the very front, but it's no use. Every time big Merle takes a step, my butt crack slides back against Blade's dick.

I won't lie. Between his arms, my spread legs, his rock-hard cock, and my pussy rubbing against the saddle, my panties are soaking wet.

I try not to even think of the night we spent licking and fucking each other into oblivion. Every sense I have is on full-tilt high alert. I'm alive out here, in the wild.

The saddle squeaks beneath me. Blade's lips rest on my hair. His chest is all muscle as it brushes my back. Fuck, he even smells like heaven, and every dicklicious naughty thought tearing through my brain is going to send me straight to hell.

If that wasn't enough, the vista splayed out in front of us is mind-blowing. I've never seen anything like this. The green rolling hills are dotted with bright purple and yellow flowers that go on forever. This has got to be the sexiest situation I've ever been in.

I'm overwhelmed, with nowhere to run. And there's no denying it—if I so much as clench my vajayjay, I'll probably come.

We get to the crest of a hill, where the view is even better than the last. I gape at a field carpeted with wildflowers of every color of the rainbow. Every time a breeze blows through it, the flowers all sway in the same direction, like a crowd of dancers glittering in the sun together, taking the same step.

Blade tugs back on the reins, bringing Merle to a stop. His broad chest presses into my back at the same time as his biceps tighten around my arms. Sparks of electricity whoosh through me as he bends closer, tickling my ear with his breath. "Isn't it pretty?"

"It is." I let my guard down a little and relax against him. I love that even though he probably sees this kind of nature wonderland every day, he's enjoying the view as much as I am.

I turn my head in the direction of his lips, wanting to tell him that, but catch myself and bring my head forward. I can't get too close to his mouth, or I'll kiss him. Probably can't look into his eyes either.

He adjusts his seat, and there's no way I can ignore his hard-on. It's like having a ham hock in my butt crack. He's so big his dick goes all the way up to my spine.

I don't know if he's trying to turn me on on purpose, but it's working. Oh, hell yeah, it is. Why did I say yes to this ride?

His mouth nestles into my hair, and I know he's going to whisper into my ear again. Tingles spray down my arms to my fingertips. I hold my breath.

"Comfy up here, next to me?" There's a lightheartedness to his tone. Something I haven't heard since our one incredible night.

I keep my body still and stare straight ahead at the magnificent view. "You seem to be more than a little bit comfortable," I tease. "If I didn't know you were a gentleman and that there's no way you'd actually be pressing your dick against a lady, I'd say you were down-right excited."

"I can't stop thinking about the way you tasted when you came on my tongue," he whispers hoarsely. "I want to fuck you so badly, Annalisa ..."

My heart races. Holy shit. I wasn't expecting him to come right out and say exactly what I'm thinking. I swallow hard as I debate how to respond, or whether I should even open my mouth. I'm afraid that once I start telling him how I really feel, I'll start tearing at his clothes. *Please, please fuck me, and don't hold back.*

I remind myself to rein it in, pardon the pun. But I could lose my job if we did anything like that again. I somehow need to defuse the situation and tell my pussy to stop aching for him. Same goes for my nipples; they need to settle the hell down before someone loses an eye and I end up filing for unemployment.

"It was your idea to come with me today, darlin'," he says, with the deepest, sexiest growl ever. "I tried to keep you away from me, but you couldn't resist me, could you?"

I laugh awkwardly, but my heart's in my throat because he's nailed it.

"Yep," I say sarcastically. "You're just too irresistible. I couldn't help myself." It would be a lot funnier if it wasn't true.

I feel his chuckle against my back, and I let out the breath I've been holding. Thankfully, he nudges Merle to start moving again, and we drop the subject. We traverse in silence through acres of golden grass and make it to the other side of the valley.

When we reach the top of the next hill, a smelly gust of wind comes from nowhere. I sniff the air. "Is that fertilizer? Did you just treat these fields or something?"

"We don't have to fertilize when the cows are grazing and the grass is high, sweet cheeks—the herd takes care of it. We're getting close to the barn. It's a big day for my girls."

Sweet cheeks? Does he mean my ass cheeks?

The trail splinters off into two, and he takes the path on the left. I can't see the herd or the barn, but the smell is getting stronger. I'm guessing they're behind the grove of trees in front of us. "So, what exactly is on the agenda today?"

"We're doing AI," he states matter-of-factly, as if I should know what he's talking about.

"Artificial intelligence?"

"Artificial insemination," he says with a chuckle. "Like I said, it's a big day for my girls. They're getting the best sperm money can buy."

I try to wrap my head around the procedure, but all I imagine is Blade's big hand going up the wazoo of some cow. I try to erase the image from my brain. "Is that something you do?"

"Hell no. No one except a highly trained veterinarian should do it. It's a delicate procedure, technically a mini surgery."

"Oh." I nod, taking it all in as we approach the trees.

"I flew Vince Moore up from Texas. He works with our cattle down there, been with my family for years. He's the best in the business."

Blade taps his boots on Merle's flank, and the horse picks up his pace. "No, darlin', if I was going to be inseminating anyone, I can guarantee you I wouldn't have to do it artificially." He laughs, and nope, I don't respond with one word about sperm, but that doesn't mean I'm not thinking about how yummy he tasted when I was giving him head. I could do it again, right this very second.

"But what's happening today isn't pleasant to watch if you're not used to it," he explains in a serious tone. "Trust me. I don't think you'd enjoy seeing it. It's messy, and you won't like the smell either."

"I'll have to agree. I'll give it a hard pass. I don't even want to think about how that needle, or whatever it is, gets in there. Besides, the cow would probably appreciate a little privacy when she's going through something so intimate."

"I'm sure the ladies will appreciate that." He laughs as we make our way through the shady grove. The cows' moos are clear as a bell now.

"We're here," Blade says softly as we approach an enormous barn. I was expecting one of those red barns you see in children's books, but this one doesn't have any walls, just a roof covering I don't know how many cows, maybe a hundred or so. The structure's the size of half a city block, surrounded by acres of pastures dotted with more cows.

Blade stops in front of a hitching post. To the left are trucks and trailers and more people than I've seen since I arrived in Montana. This is obviously where the action is. "Does the vet stay out here? Where did all these people come from?"

"We flew Dr. Moore in this morning. We don't have our airstrip yet, so he had to come in through Missoula. The ranch hands live in a bunkhouse not too far from here. It's nothing you need to concern yourself with." Blade tightens his grip around me and gets so close to me that I brace myself, hoping maybe he'll whisper into my ear again, but he doesn't.

"The last thing you need to do is get around a group of rowdy ranch hands," he says, with an edgy anxiousness. "You'll stay in my sightline today, okay? No wandering off."

"Okay." I gulp, searching around me for a band of renegade cowboys. What the hell have I gotten myself into?

"All our employees have been thoroughly checked out, but I don't know any of them personally. And I don't trust them nearly enough to be around you."

"Oh. Okay." I break into a fat smile, and even though he can't see me, I bite my lip to hide it. I like that Blade feels so protective of me. Good thing I'm not facing him, because my cheeks are burning and I know I'm blushing up a storm. "I promise I won't wander off."

"Good. Then I guess I'll have to let you down." I suck in a breath, feeling his fingers graze under my breast as he wraps his arms around my waist. "But I enjoyed the ride, my sexy Annalisa."

My Annalisa? Before I have a chance to relish that thought, Blade gets down off the horse and leaves me up here. What do I do now? I was faking it when I told him I knew how to ride. It wasn't an outright lie, but I'm guessing I haven't been on a horse for at least ten years.

"Hold on to the horn," he instructs, looking every inch like a movie-star cowboy from one of those old Westerns. His chiseled face is relaxed, as if he doesn't have a care in the world. He's obviously in his element. "Now dig your foot in the stirrup and swing your right leg over Merle. I'll be here to catch you." He flings his coat off and holds out his arms for me, and I'm drooling.

His thick biceps look like they're about to rip through his shirt. His blue eyes glisten under the rim of his hat. "Trust me," he says, grinning.

His smile. Jesus. He's so handsome it isn't even fair. But there's no doubt I trust him. Hell, after all the licking, sucking and fucking we did, I should. I take a deep breath and prepare myself. "I don't want to break my neck."

"I won't let you."

I hesitate, peering down at the drop. Blade's the judge and jury here, without a courtroom. I'll either land on my butt or in his arms, he'll decide.

"You promised, cowboy." I shift, taking hold of the horn. "Don't let me fall." I dig my foot into the stirrup and sure enough, my boot starts to slip through, but Blade's right behind me. He's holding the reins, so I know Merle isn't going anywhere. I slide my right leg up and over Merle's back and let go.

Blade's strong arms surround me in a flash. He holds me close to his broad chest and twists me. Before I know what's happening, my feet still haven't touched the ground and I'm staring into his crystal-blue eyes. I draw a breath. The way he looks at me is too intimate. I can't hide a thing from him; it's like he can see clear to my soul.

"You're mine, Annalisa," he whispers throatily against my lips.

I gasp, not knowing what to say, not believing what just came out of his mouth. My eyes grow wide, and I watch, stunned, as he brings his beautiful lips close to mine like he's about to kiss me.

"Mine." He fixes me with a stare I can't shake. "Just thought you should know." Then he loosens his hold on me, and I slide down, chest against chest, my crotch against his hard cock, until finally, I'm on my feet.

"Thanks," I say, trembling. I drop my head, too dizzy to even look at him. I know he probably has a list of women he says the same thing to, a mile long. Hell, a bazillionaire who looks like him? There's no question; there must be at least fifty—what do they call them?—buckle bunnies on speed dial.

But still. I'm so overwhelmed I can't even lift my head. Doesn't he get it? He can't throw words out like that to me. I'm not from his world. I *need* my job. I can't allow myself to be footloose and fancy-free with no repercussions. I'll pay dearly for any mistake I make the second I'm back in New York.

I let out a long breath and try to casually stretch my wobbly legs, pretending I didn't hear him. "The insides of my thighs are so sore," I say lightly. "It feels like I've been sitting on a barrel."

"It takes a bit of time to get used to." Blade doesn't seem to be feeling the aftereffects of the ride at all, nor is he the slightest bit embarrassed about claiming that I belong to him. He smiles, practically blinding me in the process, and waves to someone in the barn.

He doesn't appear to be upset about my sudden case of deafness either.

Just as I suspected. Thank God I didn't embarrass myself and respond. This is just another day at the office for him, and I'm just one of his many women.

"Come," he says, "let me show you your office for the day." We head to a small shed near the parking area. "There's a couch in there with a desk and a chair."

"Oh good," I say amiably. I swallow hard, trying to shift into business mode, but my heart is pulsing in my throat. Somehow, I need to find a way to keep it together around him instead of turning into putty every time he looks my way.

I step inside the small, rustic wood-paneled room and sigh in relief when I spot a computer. "You have internet and Wi-Fi out here?"

"Course we do." He grins. "I'm a cattleman, not a barbarian."

"Well then," I utter, scanning the room. "This is perfect. I'm all set."

"Hey," he says softly, casually running his big hand from my shoulder to my arm. His touch sets off a fire on my skin; the flame rushes straight to my pussy. I'm even wetter than I was when we were on that damn saddle together.

I try not to react to the way my body is desperate to pounce on him. I keep my face blank and just nod, like I would in a courtroom.

"I've got to go. Are you going to be okay in here? Vince is waiting for me." His blue eyes sear into mine.

Thump, thump, thump. My heart's about to break a rib. "Sure," I say, my voice high and shrill. I clear my throat. "Of course," I try again, sounding a little more like myself. "I'll be fine, go ahead. Do what you need to do."

Blade nods and saunters to the door, all sex and swagger in those jeans and boots. Then the cowboy god turns and almost knocks me off my feet again. "Oh, and it's a public computer, so no porn, okay?" He waggles his brows, lips curving into a sly smile.

"Funny." *Who needs porn with you around?* "And when you come back, you'll give me a tour of the snowmobile trails?"

"That's why you're here. Now, remember, no wandering. It's easy to get lost if you don't know the land."

I fold my arms, trying not to swoon over how protective he is. "I promise, I'll be fine."

"I'll be back to check on you in a few hours." His deep drawl hangs in the air, and damn if I don't get all tingly, taking in the sexy silhouette of his hat and the outline of his broad shoulders at the door as he steps into the sun.

It takes me a while to push Blade out of my mind long enough to focus on work. When my heart starts beating normally, I call Vivian with the cows serenading me in the background. It's hectic at headquarters, she informs me; our company has agreed to go in on another investment, this time in California, so everyone is swamped.

They don't need my assistance yet, so I dig in to the snowmobile project and draw up a draft of my proposal for the county. I might have to make a few changes after I check out the trail in person, but at least we have something to start with.

After shooting the draft over to Mr. and Mrs. Parker to look at, my slate is clear.

I've been avoiding Instagram like the plague, but I give in to temptation and check out my ex's wedding. I don't know why I scroll through all of his posts. The photos are exactly what I expected. The gorgeous happy couple walking down the aisle, their first dance, the cutting of the cake ... His parents, his sisters, the family that used to love me as their own, are all smiling, on cloud nine.

My ex looks happier than I've ever seen him, and his bride is stunning.

Now it's finally sinking in. It really shouldn't matter whether he broke up with me a week or a year before he proposed to the love of his life. The important thing is, they found each other. I stare at his over-the-moon dreamy smile. I'm happy for him—he never smiled like that at me.

We both knew deep down in our hearts that we weren't meant to be together forever. That's why we decided to end things.

Since our break-up, I've tried to put myself out there. I'd like to find my soulmate too, but I'm not holding my breath. Most of the men I've dated are either far too interested in my assets or look at me like I'm an argument waiting to happen. Let's face it, lawyers get a bad rap sometimes.

But I'm grateful for the life I have. At least my career is on track. Just because I don't have a man in my life doesn't mean I can't be happy too. I should be proud that I saved up all those years to have enough fuck-you money in the bank to pass on any case or job I don't want. And working for James Joseph Financial is my dream gig, and I don't take it for granted. Well obviously, or I would've thrown the whole thing out the window thirty minutes ago when Blade helped me down from the horse and held me.

You're mine, Annalisa. Mine.

A fresh breeze blows in through the open door, and I shut my phone off. It's too pretty a day to waste time pining over what might've been.

I scan the barn and spot Blade's brown Stetson bobbing up and down. There's a group of cowboys surrounding him, all shaking their heads like they're deep in conversation. I keep an eye on my ridiculously sexy fantasy, in sight as promised, and walk to a nearby corral.

There aren't any animals inside, but one lonely cow stands off by himself just outside the corral. He's checking me out like he's lost or something. He must've gotten separated from the herd somehow.

"What are you doing out here all by yourself, buddy?" I softly coo, keeping my distance. "You're all alone while everyone else is having fun playing in the fields." He snorts in response, and I laugh. "Or maybe you're a girl and you're upset because you're missing out on all the action. Don't worry, I don't think AI is as fun as the real thing."

I read up on black Angus cattle before I left. Most are pretty docile when they're not protecting calves. There aren't any little ones around, and I know a lonely cow when I see one. His big brown eyes look so sad. Poor thing is out here by himself, probably feels abandoned. "Are you sick?"

His eyes lock on to mine as if he wants to say something, and then he lowers his head. He seems okay, but I'm worried he'll get hit by one of the trucks coming and going.

"Stay right where you are, and I'll get some help."

Mr. Black Cow doesn't move; he's still fifteen, maybe twenty feet away. I've never been good at judging distances, but he has plenty of room to turn and bolt into the trees. He paws the ground, kicking up dirt behind him like he wants to play. He sniffs and sputters, getting himself all worked up. I'm concerned he's going to make a run for it.

"Blade," I call out, glancing over my shoulder. He's still with that group of cowboys.

I turn back to the cow. "Now, don't you go anywhere ..." I glance over again at the cowboys.

"Blade!" I yell louder. This time his hat moves as he turns and waves. I hear another loud snort. The cow is frantically pawing the ground now, making the dirt fly up and surround him in a cloud of dust. I meet his eyes again and this time see black—there is no love for me there whatsoever.

Shit. Those horns are huge. I slowly back away. "Hey, calm down," I warn, raising my hand and giving him the international stop sign. The move seems to set him off. In a flash of a second, he lowers his head like a battering ram, his massive hooves fly over the dirt, and he charges right at me.

"Fuck!" I turn, scrambling. He's moving as fast as a train, and I don't know where to run.

———— ⚬ ————

IT TAKES ME A SPLIT second to compute what's happening in front of my eyes. Annalisa might as well have been waving a red flag. The second she raised her hand, old Roger, the meanest bull on the property, set his sights on her. How the fuck did he get out? Fuck!

"Hang on, Annalisa! Don't run!" I shout. I don't know if she can hear me, but she's holding her ground. Old Roger is too—at least he's not charging anymore. They're face to face, about twenty feet apart from each other. Too damn close.

I whistle for help on the way to Merle. Grabbing my rope from the saddle bag, I quickly mount up. It's been a long time since I've done any roping, but I'm one of the best in the family.

"Heeeeyaaaah." I give out a warning call and catch Shane West's attention. I helped Shane when he inherited his new ranch, and he helped me get the lay of the land before I started my business. Shane knows his shit, and he jumps on his ride in a flash.

I give Merle a swift kick on his flanks, and he breaks into a gallop from a full stop. "Don't run, darlin'," I shout, racing to Annalisa as fast as Merle can take me. My hands clench the reins; my body's tight as a drum. And my heart. Jesus. I'd never get over it if anything happened to her.

Annalisa peeks over at me. All the color in her pretty face is gone. Unmoving, she's white as a ghost. Old Roger hasn't given up on her yet. He groans and snorts, kicking up dust.

Merle starts prancing beneath me. He knows what's up. This isn't his first rodeo. "Get to that woodpile behind you," I yell, "and stay low!"

I see the words register, but my heart stops when Annalisa braces herself like she's going to make a run for it. It's a perfectly normal reaction, but the absolute wrong move.

"Don't run," I say, keeping my voice calm. "Don't turn your back on him."

Roger lowers his head at the same time as Annalisa takes a tentative step backward. In an instant, dirt flies and all hell breaks loose as Roger goes after her again.

"Hey, bull," I shout, racing between him and Annalisa to cut off his path. Roger eyes me, and I circle his perimeter. "Over here, bull." It's enough to distract him, but now he knows he's about to be penned and makes a break for the trees. Shit.

I spot Shane in my peripheral. "Left!" I shout. "Don't let him get in those trees." Shane nods and cuts left, giving Roger a wide berth. That ornery old bull is too damn smart. He turns on his heels and charges right at full speed. I dig my heels into Merle, and we burn the breeze, catching up to him just at the tree line.

That damn bull's big ass is right in front of me. I take my shot and whip the rope over my head and throw it. "Gotcha!" I get it around his horns in one try, but now Roger's in the fight. I hold on to the saddle's horn and keep my seat. Roger bellows as he pulls and shakes his ugly head, trying to break free.

Merle stays steady, keeping up with the bull but leaving enough space between us. Next comes Shane's rope.

It takes three of us to get that nasty beast down, with two more standing by in case Roger gets loose. With Shane here, I don't need to watch every move. "You got this?" I shout. Shane gives me a nod, and I rush to find Annalisa.

"Annalisa!" I cup my hands around my mouth, directing my voice at the woodpile. "Annalisa!" I never saw her get behind the wood. I'm about to be sick. "Annalisa!" Holding my breath, I stare frantically at the stack of lumber. Finally, she pops her head up, and I let go of a long exhale. Thank God. I hurry to her.

"Are you all right?" we both shout at the same time.

The words "I'm fine" are music to my ears. I tie Merle to the fence post, and Annalisa makes her way to me, shaking like a leaf.

"You're safe now, darlin'." I wrap my arms around her and draw her close to my chest. "You're safe now," I whisper into her soft hair. Annalisa relaxes into me, still trembling and shivering.

The relief of finally holding her begins to flow through me, and that's all it takes for my cock to stand at attention.

"I—I'm so sorry. I promised I wouldn't take you away from your work." She shakes. "I-I-I'm—"

"You're about to go into shock is what you are."

She clings to me tighter, pressing her breasts against me, and goddamn I've got to be some kind of perv, because the only thing I want to do is strip her clothes off, get down on my knees and worship every inch of her with my tongue.

"I think I'm okay." Her words are all breath.

I draw back and study her. She still doesn't have any color to her face. "Let's get you off your feet," I say gently and walk her back to the office, booting the door closed behind us.

"Did you fall, darlin'? When you were running, did you bang into anything?"

She gives me a tentative smile. Her big brown eyes, usually sparkling, full of piss and vinegar, are blank. She stretches out her arms and moves her fingers. "No," she says softly. "I think I'm okay. Just got scared, that's all."

"Maybe ... but let's double-check." I squat down in front of her and grasp her right leg. She stares me down, wide-eyed. "Do you mind? I want to make sure you haven't broken anything."

She slowly nods. "But I didn't fall."

I grip her leg. The leather on her boots is so soft and light I can feel that her bone is perfectly in place. "You could've broken something bashing into the woodpile, who knows? You've got so much adrenaline rushing through you, you wouldn't feel anything." I check her other leg and knee. I straighten and run both my hands down the length of her smooth, silky right arm, then check the other.

"You're not mad at me, are you?" Her voice trembles, like she's about to cry. "I shouldn't have been—"

"You shouldn't have what, darlin'? Been walking fifty feet away from this building on a gorgeous day? Within yelling distance of about a hundred cowboys ready and able to help?"

I keep my voice even and controlled. But I'm so fucking infuriated that this happened to her on my ranch where she should've been safe. "Don't blame yourself. That's the sixth pen Roger's broken out of. There wasn't anything you could do."

"Then you're not mad that I didn't know he was a bull?"

"Mad? Hell no." I melt into her chocolate-brown eyes and run my thumb along her exquisite cheekbone. "I was scared shitless that something happened to you."

She parts her lips, and I trace my thumb down to the corner of her mouth. The heat between us is a raging furnace. I bend, slowly bringing my lips close to hers, so close I feel her breath whisper against me. And that's all it takes. My heart slams in my chest.

"The things I want to do to you ..." I confess, locked in her eyes. My fingers slide down her jaw and lift her chin, guiding her up, as I press my lips down hard on hers. I groan and bring my other hand to cradle her pretty face. My fingers tunnel in her hair.

I'm lost as I breathe in her jasmine, orange, and fucking-against-the-wall scent. I don't know if it's night or day when I kiss her, and I don't care. She parts her mouth for me, my tongue glides over the slickness of hers, and we're back to where we were that night in the hotel. Lord, how I've missed these lips.

I walk her backward to the desk, never taking my lips off her. My big hands slide over her curves and reach behind to lift her ass up on the desk. Her nipples are as big as cherries, poking against her T-shirt, just begging to be sucked. I'm ready to go apeshit, caveman style, and just rip that damn shirt off her.

"I told you you were mine, Annalisa," I growl, possessively sucking her bottom lip. "I'd hate myself for the rest of my life if anything happened to you." She gasps and digs her nails into my back, pulling me closer. My tongue snakes behind her ear. Her skin flames under my touch.

Chapter Seven

I FEEL LIKE I'M SINKING, losing all sense of me. God, I want him. I know it's wrong, but I do. My heart pounds so fast I can barely breathe.

"How long are we supposed to pretend you don't want to fuck me, Annalisa?" He groans against my lips. "I've wanted to kiss you like this the second I saw you standing in those heels in front of our office."

Office. I pull back like I've been splashed in the face with a bucket of ice water

This isn't a vacation. James Joseph Financial is paying for this trip. The hotel, rental car, everything is on their dime, including me.

I force myself to get a grip. Staring into Blade's heated gaze, so close to his lips, I tremble, searching for anything to say other than *you're absolutely correct, sir. I want to fuck your brains out.* "You mean when you saw me step in that big pile of something? Is that when you wanted to ... ?"

Did that just come out of my mouth? Bringing up a pile of poop is the best I can come up with? Really? What the hell is wrong with me?

Blade doesn't seem to care. He's still holding me, and I'm doing my best to ignore the way my heart is jackhammering.

"I was looking at your face, darlin', and your insanely hot little body," he says, coming right back to my lips. "I was so fucking hard for you, I never made it to your shoes. I was too busy thinking of all the ways I was going to fuck you."

God almighty, I've never had anyone talk to me as dirty as he does, and my pussy is throbbing for him. I can't think straight. I suck in a big breath and focus on what it would be like to be broke, with the sordid details of my shattered career plastered all over the internet.

I can see it now: *Annalisa Breckenridge Disbarred and Homeless for Inappropriate Behavior with Billionaire Cowboy Client, Blade Parker.* "We shouldn't even be kissing," I whisper, lifting my gaze to his eyes. "I want to, Blade, but it's just plain wrong."

He flinches, his baby blues bulging out of his head. "What the hell are you talking about?"

"I'm sorry." I close my eyes. This is so fucking embarrassing. "I got caught up in you." I awkwardly shift on the desk. "But you're right."

He scans me up and down incredulously. "What am I missing here?"

"When you saw me in the parking lot, you just reminded me that I was there for work and still am." I slide off the desk and get to my feet. "I didn't mean to be a cocktease. Please, believe me."

Blade's looking at me with so much disappointment that tears come out of nowhere and rush to my eyes. I blink them back and turn from him so he doesn't see. "It must've been the bull, or something. I just … forgot who I was there for a second. But you and me, like this, is such a conflict of interest."

He stares at me, unflinchingly silent. "Everything you were saying with your kisses about two seconds ago was the exact opposite of what's coming out of your pretty little mouth now."

"Are you upset?"

"You've got this whole thing backward," he hisses, pacing the room. "*You* getting hurt ..." He turns to face me, and I wish I could disappear into the floor. "Anything bad happening to you is a conflict of *my* interest, and that's a fact. As long as you're on this ranch, you're mine, and free to do whatever you want."

"You still don't get it." I shake my head. "I'm *not* free. I'm working," I sputter hopelessly.

"Do you honestly think your employer would fire you?" He raises his brows, and I can see I've completely and totally infuriated him. "I'd bury him if he said a word, darlin'. He wouldn't dare."

"It isn't just about James Joseph Financial. It's about my reputation as an attorney. I've worked so hard to protect it. How would it look if I had to fight the county, or the Bureau, and it came out that I was fooling around with a client? I wouldn't have a leg to stand on if anything ever came to court. It wouldn't be prudent for you or your family."

"I'm half tempted to kiss you into submission. I can guaran-damn-tee it wouldn't take long." He approaches me again, getting too close for my own good. I grab the edge of the desk and back against it to steady myself.

"It isn't that I don't like kissing you; it's just that I know enough to realize this kind of thing doesn't end well for girls like me. I'm the one at risk here. I—"

"Do not have all the facts." He runs a frustrated hand through his hair. "You're already talking about the ending and we haven't even started. If you ask me, you were analyzing too much when you should've been thinking about kissing."

"What?" I jerk my head back.

"You heard me, and I take full responsibility for my failure. Next time I'll kiss every damn worry out of that brilliant mind of yours. Then I'll fuck you so hard I'll leave you weak. The only thing you'll be thinking about is the next time. My cock will fuck every thought out of you."

My jaw hits the floor. My mouth is hanging open. I'm speechless, and so fucking horny I'm dripping. "You seem awfully sure of yourself, cowboy," I shoot back, the second I gather my wits.

"You're not in a courtroom, Annalisa. When it comes to fucking, you're on my turf, and we're not over. Not by a long shot."

The snowmobile trails look exactly how I imagined. There's a small road on the east side of the property, and another that cuts through the land leading to the trails. I'm not a surveyor, but it's clear the Parkers won't have to move mountains to carve out an alternate access road two miles out on the perimeter.

We ride Merle home in uncomfortable silence. I hear Blade's breath behind me and inhale his intoxicating scent the whole damn way. His body is wound up like a knot. Even his arms feel tight and angry around me as he guides Merle.

He's just as frustrated as I am. I still don't know if I did the right thing. His possessiveness makes me weak, and I ache for Blade whenever he's near me. The fire in his eyes brought me *this* close to breaking my resolve, but I had to stand firm, didn't I?

I wish that for once in my life I could've been irresponsible and gone for it. We'd probably still be fucking in the office right now. And I'm embarrassed about the whole bull incident too.

How stupid can someone be to not know the difference between a bull and a cow? I went to law school. I passed the bar, for crying out loud—I should be able to figure out something as simple as that.

Instead, I put everyone in harm's way trying to rescue me like an idiotic damsel in distress.

We don't say much when we dismount. I watch, hoping he'll say something to cut the tension, as Blade brushes down Merle. "Is there anything I can do to help?"

"Nah. I'm going to feed and water him, put him in for the night. You can go ahead and leave if you want."

"Are you asking me to go?"

"I'm just saying there isn't really much for you to do here, is all. If you want to stand around and watch, go ahead. But you never know, I could lose control and kiss you again."

I chuckle under my breath, relieved he brought the elephant in the room out into the open. "Ha, ha. Very funny," I say, wishing I could be that wild woman I was the first night we met ... "Okay." I sigh. "Well, I guess it's goodnight then."

"Goodnight," he says sharply, keeping his side to me, focused on brushing Merle's front leg.

When I get to the door, I turn for one last-ditch effort. "Blade?"

He looks up.

"I'm really sorry about the bull, and the kiss ... I care about you, I do—"

He straightens. "Save it. Have a good night."

"You too," I say softly, giving up.

I drag myself back to my trailer under a spectacular sunset of tangerine and purples. My feet feel like they're made of lead. Maybe it's all the adrenaline finally seeping out of my system. I was petrified, after all. But I doubt it.

I'm dragging because Blade and I were getting along so well, and I had to cross the line and ruin everything by kissing him again.

When he rescued me today, it was like something out of a movie. I can't even think about how damn hot it was when he jumped on that horse and lassoed the bull like a real cowboy.

I was holding my breath and creaming in my jeans the whole time. I've never seen anything so sexy or so dangerous in all my life. I thought for sure that bull was going to turn around and charge him.

When I get to my trailer, there's a note from Mrs. Parker inviting me to dinner tomorrow at their partially finished house on Wild Cat Ridge.

My heart lifts a bit at the thought of seeing Blade around his parents and getting to know them better. They really are the salt of the earth.

I'm not in the mood for eating just yet, so I fire up my laptop at the kitchenette. I leave the curtains open, hoping to see Blade when he comes back from the barn. I check my emails and see that his parents got the proposal I sent today. They give me the green light to go ahead and send it off to the county, so I polish up a few paragraphs, adding some of the details I noticed on the trail today. Then I check in with Vivian. Nothing has changed since the last time we spoke.

Now I'm bored out of my mind.

I kick back on the bed and try to get back into my romance novel, but I can't concentrate long enough to keep my eyes on the page.

Blade is all I can think about—his kisses, how protected and safe I feel when I'm with him. How perfect it was when we looked out over that field of wildflowers together today with his arms around me. How sexy that dirty mouth of his is ...

I wasn't in the wrong today, was I? They always say to listen to your heart. But what about your brain? Aren't you supposed to listen to that too?

Small-town gossip spreads like wildfire. If Blade and I got together again, I'm sure the news would be all over this tiny town in two seconds flat.

After a light dinner, I finally nodded off.

Now, I'm up with the sun again.

I take a quick shower and hurry out into the chilly air, hoping to catch Blade leaving his trailer before he heads out for the day. The tension between us is killing me. I want to apologize again, but there's no sign of him.

I scout over by the picnic table. Huck is there down by the grill and throws me a wave.

"Good morning, Mr. Parker," I call out.

"Mornin'. Pancakes are on the menu. I hope you'll be joining us."

"Oh, I will. I'll be right over in a sec." I hurry to the stables, hoping Blade's still saddling up Merle. The barn door is open but there's no sign of either of them. I poke my head into Merle's stall just in case. Nope. I blow out a sigh.

I've never been the wishy-washy type until now. I imagine this is what it feels like to be a honey bee, just buzzing around, hovering, looking for a safe place to land—in my case, it's anywhere near Blade.

Breakfast is enjoyable but uneventful, because Blade never shows.

The Parkers are sending someone over to drive me to their place tonight. Other than dinner at their house, there isn't anything pressing on my agenda, so I kill some time and take a walk after breakfast.

There's still no sign of Blade.

What am I even doing here?

There hasn't been any trouble with the transition of the property. I'm sure the county will accept our snowmobile road proposal. I'm tempted to pack my bags and drive to Missoula airport right now. I glumly stroll back to my trailer and stop.

How strange.

There's a shiny black town car parked out in front of my trailer, and standing next to it is an older man wearing a dark uniform and holding a box. I pick up my pace and hurry over.

"May I help you?"

The man graciously smiles. "Would you happen to be a Miss Annalisa Breckenridge?"

"I am." I grin, eyeing the glossy box.

"This is for you." He passes it to me.

"For me?" I've never had a package delivered like this before. "Thank you. What a surprise." My voice is about fifty octaves too high.

"Very good, miss. Have a lovely day."

He tips his hat and gets back in his car. I watch as he slowly pulls out and drives down the long, dusty dirt road.

Did my company have something to do with this? Is the county so thrilled with the idea of a new road they sent a gift? It isn't my birthday or any holiday.

I carry the box into my trailer and sit at the kitchenette.

What on earth?

I carefully untie the pretty fabric ribbon. Then I lift the top off the box and tear through all the tissue paper. There's something heavy at the bottom.

I rip through the final bit of wrapping to see ...

Cowboy boots.

I gasp as the heavenly smell of new leather fills the space. Did Blade send these?

My heart takes off in a gallop as I lift them out of the box. They're beautifully made and so soft. I run my hand over the leather, feeling the carved design on the feet, admiring the accents of turquoise. Then I check the size. Eight.

How did he know?

I feel around the tissue for a card and find nothing, but they must be from Blade. They have to be—his parents don't know I wore the wrong boots yesterday. No one knows. I didn't even mention it to Vivian.

Does this mean he's forgiven me?

I suck in a breath. God, I hope so. Or, maybe he doesn't want to ride double with me again and wants me on my own horse.

I slip out of my Ralph Laurens and angle my foot into the boots. The initials A and B catch my eye. My heart skips. They're monogramed. Did he have these custom made just for me?

Now I'm convinced Blade sent them. No one I know would ever do anything as thoughtful or as expensive as that.

My pulse races as I dig my phone out of my jeans and press his number. I can't believe he did this, and I hold my breath as I wait for him to pick up. He's probably still out with the vet, or herding cattle, or who knows what.

"Everything okay?" No greeting. No hello. Blade's deep voice hits me with a jolt, sending fluttery tingles all the way to my toes.

"Yes, everything is great. I just wanted to thank you for the boots. They're gorgeous."

"I'm glad you like them. Do they fit?" I hear mooing in the background and some kind of machinery.

"Perfectly. How did you know my size?"

His deep, throaty laugh makes me ache. "You don't expect me to give away all my secrets now, do you?"

I grin from ear to ear. "I guess not." I laugh, trying to keep the conversation where it is, light and fun.

"Well, you have a nice day." The phone crackles on his end, and I can tell he's about to hang up.

"Blade?"

"Yes?"

I want to say that I've been thinking about him nonstop. That I'm sorry I had to make things so awkward between us. That he's the best lover, and the smartest, sexiest man I've ever met, but I chicken out. "I just wanted to say ... I hope you have a nice day too. Oh, and say hi to Roger for me."

"Ha." I hear the smile in his voice. "Will do. Stay safe, Annalisa. See you tonight."

And with that, he hangs up.

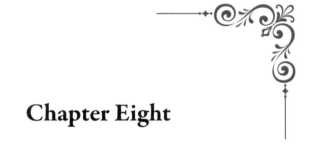

Chapter Eight

I COULD'VE LAUGHED yesterday if I wasn't so goddamned disappointed and shocked out of my mind. No one has ever turned me down before.

Doesn't Annalisa know that *I'm* the one who pushes people away?

The women I've pursued have been few and far between, but when I do pursue, I always get the woman. *Always.* And it's me who decides when to either cool it or end the relationship.

I plunge the toothpick into the middle of the brownies, trying to get my mind off Annalisa, but it's no use. When I saw her in the bar that first night, the attraction was instant and undeniable. And the way she fucked me, wild and uninhibited, left me in no doubt that our bodies were made for each other.

Now that I've gotten to know her better, she's become a fucking obsession.

Whether I'm a client or not, her job will end soon, but my feelings for her won't. I'm not about to let her slip through my fingers.

I analyze the toothpick. Perfect. It's almost clean with a few crumbs clinging to the pick. I take the pan out of the oven and set it on the counter to cool just as Mom walks in.

"Smells divine in here, chef." She gives me a peck on the cheek. "You really should sign up for one of those baking competitions. I bet you'd win."

"I don't need to enter any formal contest to know I make the best brownies in the world." I send her a wink and stroll over to the coffee pot. "Do you want a cup?"

"No thanks." She shakes her head. "Way too late in the day. I'll never sleep."

"The contractors did a nice job in here," I say, pouring a mug.

"They did." She grins, admiring her new top-of-the-line kitchen. "I can't wait until they finish the rest of the house. So, how's it going with Annalisa? I understand there was a big hubbub during the AI yesterday." She walks to the counter and inspects the brownies.

"It didn't happen near any of the girls, thankfully. Can you imagine having a bull tear through that packed barn with the vet in the middle of a procedure?"

"It wasn't Roger, was it?"

My jaw clenches and I nod. "He charged Annalisa yesterday." My blood boils with the memory. "He could've killed her."

Mom narrows her eyes. "No," she says, sounding surprised. "Sure it wasn't a bluff?"

"No, ma'am, it sure wasn't. That bull would take me out at the first opportunity. Damn thing's a liability."

I think back to the way Annalisa rested her head against me, and how relieved I felt when she was safe in my arms. Fuck. No matter how hard I try, I can't get that gorgeous creature off my mind. I was so wound up I jerked myself off thinking about her again last night.

I set my cup down and check the brownies again. "Mom?" I turn. "How did you know Dad was the one?"

She gives me a double take.

"I know you two met at a church dance." I grin, because they've told all of us the story too many times to count. "Dad locked eyes on you from across the room. You danced every dance, and that was it. You were together for the rest of your life. But you never told us exactly how you knew he was the one."

"Ah, well, let me think." She scratches her neck and leans on her new marble counter. "You know?" Her blue eyes sparkle. "I can't pinpoint the exact moment. It was just this overall feeling the moment we met. Somewhere, deep down, I just knew we'd never be apart."

"You talking about me?" Dad comes in from the hall and playfully slaps her bottom on the way to the coffee pot.

"Blade wants to know how you knew I was the one."

"Easy question. The second I saw her." He pours a cup and goes to the fridge for cream.

"The second you saw her?" I ask incredulously. "Without even talking to her first?"

Dad shrugs and takes a sip of his coffee. "Honestly, it was just a feeling I had. I mean, I didn't necessarily hear thunder or anything."

Mom wedges an elbow into his waist. He doubles over laughing. "Okay, okay ... On second thought, maybe there was thunder. And now that I think about it, there was lightning too, and then the stars fell from the sky." He turns to Mom. "That much is true, but the stars fell when I kissed you the first time."

"And that's why we named our estate in Texas 'Casa de Estrellas,'" my mother whispers. "Star house." They share such a tender, loving look that I feel like I'm invading their privacy.

"Why'd you ask?" Dad turns back to nail me. "Is there someone in particular you're thinking about?"

"No." I lie. "Just wondering. Hey, is Cash coming?" I ask, flawlessly getting him off the subject.

"Should be here any minute."

"He and the chef are still hammering out the new menu for Wild Cat Grill." Mom crosses the room to the window where the sun is starting to set behind the mountains.

I move closer for a better look at the color-washed sky. "It's kind of like being on vacation here, isn't it?"

"You're telling me," Dad chimes in. "We left a lot of drama behind in Texas. Between Houston interviewing nannies and Scarlett knee-deep in boy trouble, it's a relief to be here. Oh." His voice drops. "Did your mom tell you she's trying to talk Houston into hiring Nicky as Belle's nanny?"

"Nicolette? Billy Bowman's daughter?"

Dad nods. "Nicky needs a job, and a distraction from all that grief, to help her get back on her feet."

This is news to me, but I'm not surprised; my parents are always the first to lend a hand to anyone who needs it. They've always had a soft spot for Billy and his daughter. "Poor Nicky. She's really been through it."

"You know, we made a promise to Billy before he left for Afghanistan," Dad explains gravely. "If anything happened to him, we told him we'd look after Nicky."

Mom sighs, shaking her head. "She has no one. With her mother already gone, no siblings or grandparents, the child is on her own."

I nod. Although Nicolette isn't exactly a child—she has to be around twenty-one or two now. "She seemed to be holding up okay at the funeral."

"Well, she's not." Dad hesitates. "Nicky's in over her head trying to run her dad's old business."

"And isolating herself on that ranch." Mom narrows her eyes. "She never answers her phone. It takes days for her to even respond to my texts. But the last time I managed to get her over to Casa de Estrellas for lunch, Belle was there. Those two hit it off like two peas in a pod."

Voices echoing from down the hall make us drop the conversation. I listen for my Benson, my parent's butler. They could have a dozen staff helping out like they do in Texas, but they're going bare bones here.

Mom brightens. "That must be Annalisa."

I listen for the sound of Annalisa's new cowboy boots clicking over the hardwood floors. If she's wearing them, I'll know for a fact she's having second thoughts about pushing me away yesterday.

She wants me as much as I want her. I could hear it in the way her voice trembled on the phone today. She's just too afraid to admit it.

Then I catch myself acting like an idiot. How the hell do I know what she's thinking, and what the fuck am I doing listening for boots? When it comes to her, I've lost my damn mind.

"Ma'am, sir." Benson addresses my parents. "Your guest, Miss Breckenridge, has arrived."

"Thank you, Benson." Mom gives a satisfied smile. "Please show her in."

Benson leads Annalisa into the kitchen, and I lose my breath. My cock immediately comes alive, growing hard in seconds.

"There she is." My mother lights up and rushes over to Annalisa.

Dad grins. "Make yourself at home."

"Thank you for having me. Your home is spectacular." She sends me a shy smile and holds my gaze. But before I can get a word out, Mom swoops in on her.

"Come." She loops her hand through the nook of Annalisa's arm. "Let me show you around."

Lord, she's the most beautiful woman I've ever seen.

And what do you know?

She's wearing the boots.

Chapter Nine

MRS. PARKER TUGS ME out of the kitchen, and I get one last look at Blade over my shoulder. My heart's on a rampage at the sight of him without a hat, wearing those low-slung jeans and a T-shirt that looks like it was made to hug his biceps. All that thick brown hair that I loved running my fingers through. I can practically smell him.

"I rarely get the opportunity to have any girl talk." Mrs. Parker sends me a conspiratorial wink.

"Well, you've found the right woman." I let her lead the way down a gleaming hallway that even smells expensive. I imagine this is probably on the scale of what a hunting lodge would be. It's vast and wide; seven people could be walking beside us and not touch the wall.

"The property is far from finished," she explains. "It won't be anything like Casa de Estrellas. This has a completely different vibe."

Yeah. Like Ralph Lauren on steroids, I think to myself and follow her into a massive great room with a cathedral ceiling ornate enough for a church. A baby grand piano gleams in the corner in front of a large window. Plush leather chairs drip with luxurious furs. The four seating areas all have their own couches.

To be honest, it's a bit overwhelming. I've seen my share of glitzy digs, but nothing like this.

"This is my favorite seating area." Loretta runs her hand along the back of a deep leather couch in front of a stone fireplace that goes from floor to ceiling. The wood crackles and spits, emitting warmth, making the cavernous space seem cozy. "This is where we sit after dinner. Well ..." She shrugs. "Not all of us. Not yet."

"It's beautiful. And there's plenty of room for everyone." With a sigh, I stride over to a large picture window that looks out over a valley. Now I understand why the living room is situated in this part of the property.

From this vantage point, the scale of the rolling hills and sun-dappled valleys is breathtaking. Wildflowers dot the landscape, with mountains sparkling in the distance. There isn't another home in sight.

Loretta joins me by the window. "Nature at its finest."

I silently nod. One of the reasons I took this job with Joseph James is because the Parkers bought the acreage here mostly to preserve Montana. Their plan is to leave the majority of their property, hundreds of thousands of acres, untouched.

The community they're planning is small relative to how much land they own. They even have plans to build a hospital nearby. As it stands now, if anyone gets sick in West Palomino, if you don't call for an evac helicopter, the only medical help you can get is from a doctor who's literally called Doc. And the only way you can reach said Doc is by horse. Apparently, he treats people right at his house. I turn back to the view and watch the way the sunlight makes the mountains gleam.

"You know, it hasn't always been this way for us," Loretta says softly.

"I'm sure you worked very hard to get here."

"And we'd give all of this up in a heartbeat if it would bring back my brother- and sister-in-law."

My stomach hits the floor. I turn from the view, giving Loretta my full attention.

"I would give everything in the world for those children to have been raised by their parents. Seven children." She shakes her head sadly. "There's so much Huck's brother, Holden, and his dear wife, Nora, missed."

"I'm so sorry for your loss." I pat her arm, feeling the heavy weight of her grief. Is she saying that her brother-in-law had children also? Or are the seven children she raised actually his?" I let any trace of professional decorum go out the window and give Loretta a hug. "I'm so sorry."

Loretta studies my face. "You didn't know?"

"No. I had no idea." I'm still not exactly sure what I just heard.

"We adopted Blade, his brothers and his sister right after the accident. I thought for sure you would have read something about that."

"I mainly researched your businesses and plans for the future, to be honest. Maybe a little of your family's history ... I probably didn't go back as far as I should have." My mind races as it tries to process this horrible news.

Blade. I can't fathom what they all went through. "You lost both of them, on the same day? How devastating."

She nods solemnly and clutches her stomach as though it would physically hurt to explain.

My heart drops. "I'm sorry. I didn't mean to put you on the spot. We don't need to talk about this now."

"No. It was a long, long time ago." She lets out a labored sigh and shakes her head. "The Rio Grande had never been that high. Holden was driving; Nora was next to him in the passenger seat."

"My God." My heart is shredded for Blade. I knew there was more to him, but this? This is his history? He's far from being the typical playboy billionaire I thought he was.

"Huck and I were babysitting that day. Twenty years ago." She bows her head. "Poor Blade was so close to his mom. He was fifteen. Old enough to realize what had happened. I think the older boys felt it the worst. Little Scarlett had just turned one—she was just a baby. It was the first time in months Holden and Nora had had time to themselves. Nora was so happy they were finally having a date night."

Loretta sets her gaze out the window wistfully, lost in memories. I'm shattered for her, for Blade, for everyone. "Their car was in the exact wrong place at the worst possible time." She looks over, like I should know how bad it was, and I shake my head. I'm here if she wants to talk, but I don't want to put her through any misery on my account.

"When the river overcame its banks, there was nothing they could do. There had never been a flash flood in their location before. Their car was submerged in seconds. They were trapped inside and swept away. The velocity and impact of the water was so brutal that their car was five miles away, bashed into the side of the tree, when we finally found them."

I bring my hand up to my mouth, not believing what I'm hearing. "Horrible ... I'm so, so sorry."

Loretta reaches out and clasps my hands. "Thank you. I didn't mean to get us onto such a morose topic. For some reason I thought maybe Blade would have already told you."

Her eyes mist over. Then she swallows thickly and composes herself. What a brave woman. I wouldn't have blamed her one bit if she'd broken down in tears.

"We've all done really well." She smiles sweetly. "We're a tough team, the Parkers. We have much to be grateful for. Come," she says, holding on to my hand. "Let's join the others in the kitchen. Huck's making ribs."

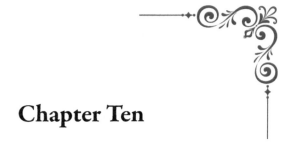

Chapter Ten

I THOUGHT HAVING HER little ass pressed up against my cock on Merle was nerve-wracking, but this ... I scan her smooth legs and lick my lips. No. Having Annalisa in my passenger seat where I can see her in that frilly skirt is worse.

My heart hammers and I clench the wheel with both hands, willing myself not to look at her again. I've got to admit, it was surprising to see her getting along so amazingly well with my family. She and Cash even fought over the last rib, like she was part of the family. A rarity.

On the few occasions when I've introduced a woman to my parents, it ended the relationship. The second I pulled up to our estate in Texas I could see the wheels spinning, like my family was a jackpot at a casino, something to win.

With some women, it's all about the money. They've got dollar signs in their pupils under all those false eyelashes.

But not Annalisa. If one hundred and sixty thousand acres doesn't make her look at me like I'm a cash prize, I'm not sure anything will.

She interrupts the silence. "Thanks for the boots." I glance over to see a slow smile spread across her face.

"Glad they fit."

She stretches out her legs and rolls her ankles, admiring her gift. "You even had them monogrammed for me."

"I didn't want you to forget who gave them to you." I keep my eyes on the windy curve.

"I'd never forget the cowboy who saved me from the bull."

"And fucked you in a bar bathroom, and then in the shower, the bed, on the floor, against the wall and ... almost on top of a desk. But the night is still young." My cock twitches with hope, but after her rebuff in the office, I'm letting her come to me this time. And I know she will. It isn't a matter of *if*, only *when*.

Annalisa's eyes grow wide. She holds my stare for a split second before she primly straightens her skirt and tugs the hem over her knees. Okay, now I hate that skirt. As soon as she gives me the opportunity, that skirt is the first thing coming off.

"I had a good time tonight," she says sweetly, having no idea that my brain is now fully entrenched in the gutter. In my mind I'm running my tongue over her clit and lapping up her sweet pussy juice. "Your brother Cash is something."

I glimpse over at her. "That he is ..." If Cash had been the one to give Annalisa the tour, I'd probably never see her again. I'm only half-joking.

We reach our trailers after ten minutes of small talk, and there's part of me that doesn't want to get out of the car. I like it like this, when it's just the two of us and she can't run anywhere.

But I open her door and help her out of the car. Her hand feels like velvet against my callouses. I'm still holding it when she's on her feet, and I don't want to let go. Not ever.

She sets her sparkling eyes on me, and I can see the flames flicker in those mysterious dark eyes of hers. The air is thick and molten, just waiting to catch fire.

Even if we hadn't fucked the first night, the raging attraction between us would still be there. Any time. Any place. I have no doubt about it whatsoever.

I wish she'd stop denying herself and trust me.

Don't get me wrong, I understand how worried she must be after how hard she's worked to get where she is. But I wouldn't allow anyone to hurt Annalisa professionally, or in any way whatsoever. I'm not the kind of douchebag to threaten anyone with my wealth, but I'm not afraid to use my power and resources to defend the people I care about.

"Thanks for the ride," she says nervously. Her pink tongue darts out to swipe her lips. She draws her hand back to her side. "This is me." She points to the trailer. "I know you have to get up before the sun, so ..."

"We should have a nightcap." She twists her head and gapes at me. "Options, darlin'. We have options." I didn't hire the best ranch manager in the country to have to babysit him twenty-four-seven.

"You don't have to get up?"

"I'm always up for you." I send her a grin and she laughs. The problem is, I'm not joking. I was hard for her the second she arrived at my parents' place.

"You," she coos teasingly. Her silky voice hangs in the sultry air. "You just don't give up, do you?"

"I take it that's a yes?"

Annalisa bites her lip and pretends to give it some thought, but I know she's been creaming in her panties for me. She just won't admit it. "Okay, cowboy."

"Keep calling me cowboy and I might not be able to hold myself back."

She cocks a brow.

"The whiskey's in my trailer. Want to come in?"

"No, no, no, no," she says. "I'll wait out here."

"Be right back." I head to the trailer and remind myself she's playing ping-pong in her head again. One wrong move and she'll run for the hills.

There's a fully stocked bar in here, but I grab the whiskey bottle and two glasses. I poke my head out the door, just to be sure. "Whiskey okay? I've got wine too."

"I want to be a cowgirl tonight." She smirks and wiggles her foot, showing off her new boots. "Bring on the whiskey, pardner."

God, she's adorable, just begging for trouble. And I'm happy to oblige. I hurry out the door, and we stroll side by side to the Adirondack chairs in front of the old oak.

Annalisa takes a seat while I light the fire pit to the sound of crickets chirping in the surrounding fields.

I pour our drinks and sit beside her, handing her the glass. Her face glows in the firelight as she takes it and holds it up to mine. "What should we toast to?"

"Sugar whiskey." I click my glass against hers and wait for her reaction.

She wrinkles her nose and peers into the glass. "Did you put sugar in here?"

"No, Annalisa." I chuckle. "Sugar whiskey is your nickname." I take a sip of the smooth liquid gold and lean back in the chair. "That's what I called you that first night we met when I didn't know your name."

Her eyes blaze into mine and she holds back a smile. "But why sugar whiskey?"

"You sure you want to know?" I cock my brows.

She smirks. "Tell me."

"Because your kisses tasted like whiskey, and I knew your pussy would taste like sugar." She squirms under the heat of my gaze, blushing up a storm. "And I was right. You have the sweetest pussy on the planet. So the name suits you, doesn't it?"

"Um ..." She bites her lip, doing everything she can to keep a straight face. "I'm not sure 'sugar whiskey' is the proper way to address a business associate."

"I think we're way past being business associates by now, darlin'. Don't you?" I set my glass down and catch Annalisa staring off into the fire, probably too embarrassed to say a peep. "Hey," I say softly. "Look at me."

She turns, quizzically scanning me. Her brown eyes have those gold flecks in them tonight, and I'm entranced as usual.

"If you'd give me another thirty seconds, Annalisa, I promise we can be whatever you want us to be."

She studies me silently and looks off into the distance again, like she has to really think about what she's going to say next. Okay. Now I'm concerned. I haven't seen that expression on her before.

"Blade," she says in a low, serious tone. "Your mom told me what happened to your parents tonight." Her eyes start to water. "And I'm so sorry."

My heart drops, and I'm catapulted back to the hazy memories of my mother and father, the goddamn horror of the accident, how my life turned to a living hell in an instant. "I think I'm changing your nickname." I keep my voice light to cover the hurt. "I'm going to call you buzz-killer from now on."

"I'm sorry." She reaches out and caresses my arm. "I didn't mean to be a downer, I just wanted you to know that I knew. Why didn't you tell me?"

"I wasn't trying to keep any deep dark secret from you. I thought everyone on the planet knew by now."

"Well, I didn't. And I'm sorry. That must've been awful for you."

"It was." I sigh and take another sip of whiskey. "Tell me this. Does it change the way you think of me?"

"No." She shakes her head. "Not really." She takes a deep breath. "I lost my dad, so I know what it's like to lose a parent. I'll never get over it, so I can only imagine what you went through losing both your mother and father at such a young age."

I study her expression, reading the depth of her pain clearly. "I'm sorry you lost your father, Annalisa." I unconsciously reach out and hold her hand. "It's a shitty thing to go through at any age."

She nods, not pulling away. "It gave me a different perspective of you," she says softly.

"How so?"

She blinks. "Well, that kind of loss really changes you, you know?"

I sigh. "Don't I."

"It makes your heart a little more guarded."

"I never thought about it like that, but you're right."

"So maybe when you said you thought we could be more than just a one-night stand, you were serious." She bites her lip and gazes over the grassy field at the old oak.

"Hell yes, I was serious. I still am," I say, surprised she didn't believe me.

"Maybe after everything you've been through, you're not the kind of man who plays games after all, and maybe you really do like me."

What is she saying? I let go of her hand and set my glass down. "Like?" I get up and squat in front of her chair so she can see my face and know I'm dead serious. "I'm fucking head over heels for you, baby. You're all I think about."

She peers down at me with furrowed brows. Her lips are tight with worry. "I thought, maybe you, you know ..." She hesitates. "Were playing the field. I wouldn't judg—"

"Hell no. Don't believe all the bullshit they write about the Parker brothers. I haven't been with anyone in a long time. I broke up with my last serious girlfriend over a year ago." I rest my hands on her silky thighs, just above her knee.

"What happened?"

"It's a long story and I don't want to get into it. Bottom line is I almost got taken to the cleaners. She had someone on the side, and they were both after my money." I laugh sarcastically. "It was all about the divorce settlement and we weren't even engaged. What about you?"

"Me?" She brings her hand to her chest as if she's honestly surprised I would ask such a thing.

"Yes, you. You're a once-in-a-lifetime woman. Why hasn't a catch like you been taken?"

She laughs. "I'm more of a catch-and-release." She sighs. "I think my ex dated me to find out what he didn't want. He proposed to the first girl he met about a week after we broke up."

"That was so *I* could meet you, darlin'." Instinctively, my hand glides up her satin leg, and I catch myself before my fingers climb under her skirt.

Instead of brushing me aside, Annalisa breaks into a devilish smile and bends so we're eye to eye.

"You think so?"

I creep close to her lips. "I *know* so."

She closes the space and kisses me. Soft and smooth, her warm velvet lips press to mine, making my chest tighten and my cock swell.

I cradle her face in my hands and kiss her gently at first until, fuck, I'm home again. I take what's mine. The fire roars through my blood as I kiss her hard and hungrily, so she'll never forget who she belongs to.

"Blade," she whispers, lifting off the chair and pressing me down on the cool grass until she's on top of me. Fuck, she's so full of surprises. I rake my hands over her curves, drinking in the sight of her in the moonlight.

She brushes my hair back over my forehead and peers at me like I'm dessert, and something about it makes me hit the brakes. My hands slide up the soft flesh of her arms. "What happened to your conflict of interest? Not that I'm complaining."

"You." She bites her bottom lip mischievously. "You were right. I was thinking too much in the office."

"In all fairness, you were charged by a bull and more than a little rattled."

"And the county responded to my proposal about an hour after I sent it." She grins. "They loved the idea, so there won't be any litigation."

"And?"

"And I won't be around forever." She cocks her head, and the corner of her lip turns into a half-smile. "Besides, you're irresistible."

I don't argue with her about not being here forever. She doesn't know it yet, but I'm never letting her go. "So, I'm irresistible, am I?"

"Uh-huh." She presses her hands on my chest and scrambles to her feet.

"Where the hell are you going?

"I think I'm buzzed." She giggles. "I finished that whole glass of whiskey while we were talking, and it just hit me like a ton of bricks." She laughs and takes off for the oak tree. I'm still on my back and get a flash of pink panties as she runs. Now my cock is ready to shoot its load.

I get to my feet as Annalisa grabs the ropes of the tree's swing and pulls it back to her. She's at the top of an incline and uses the height to get on the wooden slat. "C'mon, what are you waiting for, cowboy?"

You. For my entire life. Her wish is my command. I stroll to the oak, watching as she digs her boots into the dirt and pushes off.

Her long satiny legs fly up as she pumps the air and swings higher.

Holy hell. She's killing me here.

"Push me." She giggles. "I want to go higher." She swings her legs, and I swear to God, as pretty as her face is, the only thing I see are creamy thighs and easy access to what's under that frilly skirt.

I probably feel the way old Roger did. I *want* this woman. I *crave* this woman. Not to charge, but to take and mount. I might as well be digging my hooves into the soil and snorting. Annalisa's eyes meet mine—without a doubt she knows what's coming, and she wants it too.

She skims the dirt with her heels, slowing herself down. Both hands are still hanging on to the rope on either side of her head, making her tits jut out. Her nipples poke through the fabric of her blue blouse clear as day. Her skirt is hiked up on her thighs.

I stand in front of her, grab the ropes just above her hands, and tug. She swings forward, spreading her legs to accommodate me. She's high enough off the ground that her pussy is right around the same height as my throbbing cock. I tug the rope again and pull her flush against me so she can feel how crazy I am about her.

"No more games, Annalisa." I bring my hand to her jaw, brushing my lips over hers in the softest kiss. A warning. "No more fucking games."

Her breath hitches. "No," she whispers dazedly.

"No?" I pull back.

"No more saying no." She lets out a soft, fluttery moan and lets go of the ropes. I half expect her to break away, but she doesn't. Annalisa wraps her hands around my neck, draws me closer to her lips and kisses me hungrily.

Her legs tighten around my thighs as my tongue snakes into her mouth and greedily finds hers. I bring my hand to her breast and find her taut nipple with my thumb. She lets out a soft gasp that almost makes me come in my pants. My pulse races in a blinding-hot chemical reaction.

All bets are off.

Tracing down the outline of her breasts with my fingers, I travel down the body I've craved since the second I saw her. Her jasmine-and-orange scent surrounds me. The grip of her legs loosens as I move down to her skirt, transfixed at the sight of her. Legs spread, sugar-cube nipples, she's mine for the taking.

"Grab the ropes," I grunt, squatting, keeping my eyes on the prize. Annalisa holds on as I tug her skirt up out of my way. I spread her silky legs around my neck and grab the swing, pulling her to my mouth.

Fuck. I close my eyes and inhale the pussy I've missed so much. She's so sopping wet there's a dark stain under my lips, and I lick right up over it through her sticky panties, making her yelp.

Her thighs tremble as she presses herself against my lips, begging me to get inside her slick little cunt with my tongue. "You like fucking my mouth, don't you, sugar whiskey?" I nibble her soaking panties, raking my teeth gently over the fabric, teasing her hard little nub as my raging cock bangs against my zipper. "You're so fucking wet for me," I groan. I slip my fingers into the side of the barely there fabric and spread her honey over her clit.

Annalisa cries out. Her hand comes down on my shoulder.

"Hold the rope with both hands, baby," I moan in ecstasy, smelling her nectar, making tight circles around her clit with my thumb. "I'm going to make you come so hard you might fall."

Nothing can stop me from inhaling every inch of her. My hungry cock is leaking cum, clamoring and aching to ravage her snug little heaven.

I rip her panties with my teeth like a fucking savage and tug the swing so she's right against my face. I lap up and down, greedily, slurping up her warm liquid sugar and slick velvet skin. Annalisa lets out a shriek and bucks against my tongue.

I'm obsessed with the taste of her. Lost in her whimpers and gasps, I lick her pretty wet slit and groan. She's even sweeter than I remember—a straight sugar rush, a liquid high. I could live on her nectar alone.

"Spread your legs wider, Annalisa." I rock the swing, moving her against my mouth.

"Shit," she yelps, shuddering. "Oh my God. That feels so good."

"No more saying no." I tease her clit with the tip of my tongue, and she cries out into the night. Finally, her guard is down, and her lust for me is unleashed. She's not holding back from me any longer, and she's even more beautiful than the first time. My heart pounds as I keep the swing steady, hungrily lapping her up and down.

"Fuck!" she screams. "You're going to make me come." Her skin's on fire as she rolls her hips, fucking my face faster and harder, her legs tightening around my neck.

Burning red lust pours through my veins, consuming me with an uncontrollable need. Covered in her juice from my nose to my chin, I shove my tongue inside her slippery hot glove. Annalisa lets out a throaty moan, and I know she's close.

"Come for me, Annalisa." I tug the base of the swing and rock her faster with one hand, while bringing the other to her ass. I wrap my lips around her clit and suck, holding her there. Her thighs shake and clamp around me.

"Fuck," she screams, coming unraveled, and the sound of her pleasure is pure bliss.

"That's it, baby." I lick and suck her trembling pink button. She shudders and spasms, and I stay with her, holding her close, fucking her with my tongue, keeping the pressure on until she shatters against me.

"Oh my God," she says softly, giving me a lazy smile. The second I straighten, she lets go of the ropes and falls into my arms.

"Do you know how beautiful you are when you come?" I hold her close as my cock pulses against her. "I swear, I could live between your legs." I gaze into her eyes, still amazed that I found such a woman. Gorgeous, smart, grounded, and sexy beyond words. I didn't think anyone like her existed outside of a fantasy.

"If you're not careful, you're going to turn me into a sex-crazed maniac, cowboy," Annalisa whispers, and before I can say another word, she presses her lips on mine and we're on the grass, trying to rip each other's clothes off. She climbs on top of me and takes hold of my belt buckle.

"This needs to come off," she gasps between kisses.

"I couldn't agree more." In seconds, I toss my jeans off to the side and my cock lurches free.

Her eyes lock on to the sight. I'm hard and needy; my dick drips pre-cum, practically reaching for her.

"Is that for me?" she asks, her eyes darkening with desire.

"It's all for you. Every inch of it."

Annalisa gives me a sly grin and stretches out on her back. She lifts her skirt, seductively spreading her legs for me. The sight of her pink pussy glistening in the moonlight sends my cock into a rage. I growl like a fucking animal and crawl on top of her, torrents of fire tearing through my system. It's all I can do to hold myself back and be gentle and not pin her to the ground with my throbbing rod.

"I'm going to fuck that exquisite little pussy of yours raw," I whisper against her mouth, rubbing my cock over her clit. Annalisa moans. "Would you like that, sugar whiskey?" I claim her lips as my thick dick prods at her opening.

"Yes." Pleading into my eyes, she tilts her hips up for me. "You already know I'm safe. Fuck me raw. I want to feel all of you."

"Are you saying you want me to fill your sweet little pussy with my cum?" I stroke my cock over her wet folds.

"Please," she pants.

And that's all it takes. I push into her snug opening, feeling warm velvet resistance. She's like a vise around me. I groan as I slide in another inch and her folds slowly open.

"Is this what you want?" I push in deeper, kissing her, letting her get used to my size again.

"Yes." Annalisa spreads her legs wider, and I sink deeper into her. "Fuck yes." She rocks with me, moaning against my lips. We find our rhythm, and I'm lost in her pussy's tight grip. Annalisa clings to me deep inside as I claim her, gliding in and out, taking her harder and faster.

My pussy. My lips. My woman. Mine ...

My cock is insatiable, blinded by the need for more. "I'll never get enough of you. Never."

"Fuck me, Blade," she chokes out. "Harder."

I'm in another world, scorching with the raw lust of an animal. Our grunts and moans ring out into the dark as we mate each other in the grass.

"Blade," she cries. She tugs my face down to her lips and kisses me in a frenzy. My tongue finds hers and she sucks it greedily, wrapping her legs around my hips to urge me in as deep as I can go.

"Ride my cock, Annalisa." I don't recognize my own growl. I slide my hand down her smooth belly and roll her clit under my thumb. "Fuck me, sugar whiskey. Milk me dry."

She screams and lifts off the ground, clinging to me and shaking. "Oh God." Her nails dig into my back as she fucks my dick faster.

"Christ," I grunt, sucking her neck so hard I know I'll leave a bruise. Coated with her cream, I pump into her harder, moving her on the grass with the force.

"Yes!" she pants. Our bodies slap together; my balls bang against her ass.

I increase the pressure with my thumb, circling her slippery clit. "Come on my big cock, baby. Cover me with your cum." Her pussy tightens around me. My balls are about to explode as I thrust into her.

"Fill me. Come inside me." She shakes, bucking and spasming around me.

"Fuck, Annalisa," I roar. Shattering, I unleash my seed, drilling it deep inside her womb and quenching every need or want she's ever had.

We hold each other, panting and clinging to each other after our storm.

I close my eyes and kiss her tenderly until we collapse on the grass, waiting for our heartbeats to normalize.

"Are those headlights?" Annalisa asks.

"What?" I turn in the direction of the driveway.

We both hear the car's engine at the same time and freeze, staring at each other.

"Shit. My parents are back."

We scramble to our feet, half laughing and half freaked out. Annalisa pulls the hem of her skirt down so she's covered. I help straighten her blouse, with my bare ass howling at the moon.

She tosses me my jeans and I have them zipped in seconds. I grab her hand, and we make a run for it back to the trailers.

"Wait." Annalisa skids to a stop. She turns around and makes a beeline back to the swing, pulling me with her.

"What is it?" She lets go of my hand to frantically search the grass.

"My panties." She giggles. "They've got to be here somewhere."

Chapter Eleven

I WAKE TO THE SOUND of Annalisa's soft exhale. With her warm back to my chest, I cradle her, gently pulling her closer under the comforter. She stirs, snuggling her ass against my morning wood. As much as I want to plunge inside her sweet pussy, I don't wake her.

I'm content just lying here with her in my arms. If I've learned anything in my thirty-five years, it's that if there's an emptiness inside you, all the toys, the planes, the latest Bugatti, the seaside property, the yachts, whatever money can buy, won't fill the emptiness.

And that's what's crazy about this thing we have—I don't feel empty. From the first time I held her, I felt a contentedness I haven't experienced before. I've slept like a baby both times we've spent the night together.

Her phone rumbles on the table beside us. Annalisa lets out a sigh and sleepily rolls over, finding my lips. "Good morning, cowboy." She kisses me softly and grins.

Whoever's calling gives up, and the phone goes silent.

"Sleep well?" I snuggle into her neck and suck.

"It's like I never slept." She giggles. "I was with you in my dreams all night."

"Do tell." I kiss her tenderly, relishing her sleepy taste.

"We just continued what we were doing before we fell asleep," she says coyly.

"I think we were talking about how I'm never letting you out of my arms again." I crawl on top of her and make a trail of open-mouth kisses down her cheek to her neck.

"Hmm," she drowsily moans. "I like the sound of that."

"Is this what we were doing?" I tease, kissing all the way down to her nipple. She shivers under my mouth.

"Hmm ... I think so, but I can't be sure." She arches her back, and I circle her dark pink areola with my tongue. "Yes, I think that's it."

"This?" I wrap my mouth around her left nipple and suck. I'm dripping pre-cum on her warm thigh.

"Yes that's it," she says, sliding her hand between us. "But I was doing something else." I groan as her velvet hand finds my cock. "Yes," she whispers throatily, "it's all coming back to me now." Annalisa squirms underneath me. Gripping my shoulders, she playfully rolls me over so she's on top.

"Now where was I?" Her long brown hair sways against me, tickling my chest as she crawls like a tigress with her sweet bare ass up in the air.

I give it a light slap. She turns and grins before setting her sights on my aching cock. It isn't hard to find because it's as thick as a baseball bat, standing straight up and pointing at the ceiling.

The morning light seeps through the curtains, casting a soft yellow glow around her. She wraps her silky hands around my dick and eyes me temptingly. She looks as hot as sin.

"Fuck." I flinch the second her lips wrap around my crown. And strike me to hell, I want to fill that sexy mouth of hers with cum and watch it drip down her chin.

"Annalisa," I hiss, choking out the fucking words, captive between her lips. Her moan vibrates through me as she strokes all the way down and back up, coating every inch with saliva and pre-cum.

My heart races as I move my hand down and grab a fistful of her thick hair. I hold it out of the way, watching her mouth stretch around my veiny cock. *Fuck.* My eyes roll into the back of my head as she slurps, swirling her tongue around my shaft, licking and sucking me like a damned lollipop.

Then she drags her eyes to mine and locks on with a fiery gaze. Her small hands wrap around me as she jerks my cock faster before she licks and sucks me again.

"Hmm," she groans, with my enormous dick down her throat. How did I get so fucking lucky? She keeps the pressure tight around me, sucking me up and down.

"Jesus, that feels amazing." I thrust up, rolling my hips. My abs are as taut as a drum and my body's about to snap. I guide her head down and up, never taking my eyes off her as she fucks me with her mouth, just the way she did that first night, only better. It's like I have my own fucking porn star here.

My ass clenches, and my dick throbs under her expert tongue. My heart feels like it could break through my rib cage as Annalisa slides a hand around my heavy aching balls and squeezes with just the right amount of pressure. "Fuck, baby, just like that ..." My muscles harden as I hold back, trying to make the indescribable pleasure last before I pump her sweet little mouth with my dirty seed. But I'm right on the edge.

She sucks me harder, with quickening strokes. "Fuck my mouth, Blade," she purrs. I'm so far down her throat she can barely get the words out.

I roll my hips, pistoning into her mouth.

"Give it to me, cowboy." Her needy voice rips through me. "Give me all that cowboy cum." She licks and sucks, clutching my aching balls, and the bomb goes off. I'm hurled into the unknown as the ecstasy explodes inside me.

"Fuck," I shout. "Fuck!" The orgasm rips through me as my cum shoots into her mouth, going off in spurt after spurt as she swallows every drop. "Jesus." I relax back down on the bed, panting, my pulse tripping through my veins.

Annalisa crawls up next to me with a grin from ear to ear.

"You." I chuckle. "You're like a drug. You should definitely come with a warning." She raises her brows and runs a finger down my chest.

"And what would that warning be?"

"Caution: Do not operate heavy machinery. Highly addictive." I laugh and pull her into my arms. She snuggles into my chest, and I run my fingers through her long silky hair. "What am I going to do with you?" I sigh, still breathing heavily.

"I'm sure we can think of something."

My cock twitches, coming up with a few ideas of its own, just as her damn phone starts vibrating and banging on the table beside us.

Annalisa rolls her eyes. "That's the second time. It might be work."

"They call you on the weekend too?"

"What's a weekend?" She scrambles off me and checks the number. "It's the office. Sorry."

"Don't be." I give her a kiss and crawl out of bed. "I'm going to hit the shower," I whisper. "Join me when you're ready."

"It's a date, cowboy." She gives me one of those smiles that takes my breath away and presses the button on her phone. "Hey, Vivian. What's up?"

I NEVER GOT TO JOIN Blade in the shower because Vivian kept me on the phone for an hour, updating me on the new office complex we're financing in California. By the time I finished, Blade was up on Wild Cat Ridge trying out a possible lunch menu with Cash, and I didn't have the heart to interrupt him.

I took a quick shower but have spent the whole day in yoga pants and a sweatshirt, working at my computer. My heart is so heavy, though, I can barely concentrate. I didn't plan for this to happen and sure didn't count on falling for Blade like this.

Now I have to put my big-girl panties on and buck up somehow. My company needs me in California.

Ugh. How am I going to do this? I thought we'd have the full seven days together, but because everything went so smoothly with the county, I have to leave tomorrow. Blade texted me a few minutes ago. He's on his way and should be here any minute.

I save my work and shut down my laptop. Then I run a brush through my hair and put on some lipstick, trying to make myself presentable. I wish I could go back in time to yesterday and just stay there forever.

When I hear Blade's knock, my heart skips. I almost dread letting him in, but I have to break the terrible news. I take a deep breath, open the door and swoon. God dang, I'll never get used to how gorgeous he is.

He's wearing a blue button-down shirt that makes his eyes sparkle like jewels. His chiseled face is perfection under that hat as he steps into the trailer all fresh and breezy. There's that hypnotic leather-and-cashmere smell again ... Oh, how I adore that smell.

"I missed you, cowboy." Grinning, I get up on tiptoes and kiss him. His big strong arms wrap around me, and he lifts me off the ground in a hug.

"Feeling is mutual, sugar whiskey," he says in a deep throaty voice. His blue eyes sparkle into mine and I'm snared. He might as well have thrown a rope around me and lassoed me like he did old Roger. I could stand here and stare at him for hours.

"For you." He hands me a small box. "It's chocolate. The chef whipped up a soufflé for dessert."

"Thanks," I say, trying to be light and casual. We sit at the kitchenette and I open the box. Blade peeks inside.

"The chef was beside himself when I asked him to wrap it up for you. He said it might drop, but it looks like it held up pretty well."

Under usual circumstances I'd be giddy as hell over this, but Blade's good mood only makes me feel sadder. How am I going to tell him? How am I going to get through saying goodbye?

"There's a spoon and napkin in there." He points with a smile. "Go for it."

"Thanks. If there was ever a day I needed chocolate, it's today."

"Hard day, huh?" His eyes fill with concern.

"Yeah," I say, not sure when or how I'm going to tell him. There's no backing out on going to California either, because Vivian booked my ticket an hour ago. "I spent all day on the computer. So this will really hit the spot." I dig into the gooey chocolate and take a bite of nirvana.

Blade stares, waiting for my reaction, and I force myself to smile. "I think this is the best thing I've ever tasted in my life." *Well, except for when I sucked your cock this morning.*

I sigh, trying to embrace the fact that my fantasy is over. I can't hold it in any longer. I purse my lips in a grimace.

"What is it?" He reaches for my hand, and my stupid chin starts trembling. I'm afraid that if I look at him, I'll burst into tears like an idiot, so I stare down at the dessert.

Blade's big hand comes under my chin and tilts it up, forcing me to meet his gaze. I gulp. Might as well get it out of the way. "Do you want the good or bad news first?" I let out another heavy sigh.

Blade cocks his head and gives me a once-over. "Hit me with the bad. Let's get it over with."

I scoop into the soufflé and get a spoonful. Then I glide it to his beautiful mouth like an airplane to feed it to him. He raises his brows before he opens his mouth. "For reinforcement," I clarify and wait for him to swallow. "I'm needed in California."

He narrows his eyes. "Okay."

"No." I shake my head. "Not okay. I don't get to stay for seven days. My company cut my trip short and I have to be on a plane tomorrow." I point to my luggage. "I was just packing."

He checks out my bag, trying to process the news. "Leaving tomorrow, after I finally find you? No." He shakes his head defiantly. "I'm sorry, but that's impossible. You're not leaving."

"I know, it's awful, but I have to. The good news is your parents and the county are getting along like gangbusters. You can start building that access road immediately."

"Why do I suddenly not care about those damned snowmobiles?"

I rub his arm and then reach across the table and kiss him. "I know, I know. I sort of don't care anymore either." I glumly stick my spoon back into the soufflé and take another bite. "The chocolate isn't helping my mood much. Don't get me wrong," I quickly add. "It was sweet of you to bring it."

Blade lets out a beleaguered sigh. "We don't have our airstrip built yet. We don't even have our copter here. I'm sorry."

I tilt my head and study his beautiful blue eyes, wondering why on earth he's apologizing. "What does that have to do with us? I mean, you know you don't have to try to impress with your money. I'd lo—like you just as much if Merle was your only mode of transportation."

He chuckles. "I wasn't trying to impress you with my money, darlin'. I can think of a lot better ways to do that ..."

"No doubt." I laugh, digging into the soufflé again. "Just wanted you to know, I'm not one of those gold diggers." I meet his eyes again. "I have my own money and can take care of myself."

"I know very well that you're your own woman, sugar whiskey." He grins. "It's just one of the many, many qualities I admire about you. You're fully independent and in no need of a man."

Hold on. I immediately backtrack. "But that doesn't mean I don't *want* one. A man, I mean. You as my man."

Chapter Twelve

BLADE AND I SPEND OUR last night together making love through the night, and it was love. Still wild and crazy, but more tender too. I can't speak for him, but the sex felt different last night, like we were connecting on a deeper level.

And now, I can't imagine how I'll ever say goodbye to him. How am I going to get through the next few hours? I had to hide in the bathroom this morning so he wouldn't see me crying. Now, there's a lump the size of his belt buckle lodged in my throat, and I'm not even at the airport yet.

At least we're spending every last second we have with each other. We're holding hands in the back seat of the same town car that was parked in front of my trailer the day Blade sent me the boots. Turns out the driver's name is Timothy, one of the Parkers' right-hand men in Montana.

Someone else is returning my rental for me. It's a little strange to have anyone helping me. It's completely out of my comfort zone to hand over any of my responsibilities.

If the car isn't returned on time, or if anything happens to it, I'm liable. But I trust Blade. He said I didn't have to worry about the car, and he was right. I called the rental office and the car was returned, spotless and with a full tank of gas, at five thirty this morning.

"I'm going to miss you," I say softly and squeeze his hand.

"I haven't gone anywhere yet." He chuckles. "Hungry?" I frown, side-eyeing him. Blade's awfully chipper considering I'm about to be long gone.

"Yeah. I guess I am, now that you mention it." I close my eyes, remembering how as soon as I admitted that I was falling for him and could see him as mine, we spent the whole night in bed. We had chocolate and popcorn for dinner.

"Me too." Blade sends me a panty-melting grin and pulls out his phone. His fingers fly over the keyboard, and I turn to the window. My nose is pressed to the glass, my heart flipping and flopping in my stomach. We zip past brown rolling hills with a scattering of trees. My pulse thuds in my ears as we get closer and closer to my impending doom.

I gasp, swallowing that thick lump down my throat. There it is—the Missoula International sign. I turn to Blade, who gives me a way too pleasant, drop-dead gorgeous smile, and I go back to looking out the window.

I hold my breath as Timothy turns the wheel and we enter the airport grounds. Missoula International isn't very large, and the building immediately comes into view. I think back to the day I landed.

It was only a few days ago, but it feels like it's been a year, so much has changed. I grab my purse off the seat, bracing for when the car pulls up—and we whiz by the building. "That's me." I turn, looking out the back window. I tug Blade's hand. "Are you going to tell Timothy we just drove by the entrance?" I whisper.

Blade sends me a mischievous grin and leans close to my ear. My heart skips at the nearness of him. "Trust me?" he asks.

I nod. "Of course. But—"

"Don't worry, darlin'." His eyes twinkle as his lips turn up in a sly smile. "You'll get to California on time."

Wha? I twist back to the window, keeping my eyes peeled. Where on earth are we going? Is Timothy going to turn the car around? Now we've passed the entire airport complex. We're on some side road leading to—

A small landing strip comes into view, with a plane parked beside it. Timothy pulls the car off the side road and drives straight to the plane, then cuts the engine.

"What's going on?" I whisper again, my heart pounding a mile a minute.

"This is your ride, sugar whiskey." Blade laughs. "God, are you fun."

Timothy gets out of the car and opens my door. "Miss?" He extends his hand, and I gawk at the gleaming white plane behind him.

"Thank you. One sec, please." I tun to Blade, who's smiling down on me from under the brim of his hat. Even through its shadow I see his blue eyes sparkle with mischief. I point to the plane. "Am I flying in that to California?"

"*We*, darlin'. *We* are flying in that to California."

My heart leaps and I try to process what's happening. "We?"

"If you have to go to California, I'm going with you."

I narrow my eyes at him. What did he just say? The words and letters all bang against each other in my brain until, like a game of Scrabble, the words fall into place.

What?!" I jump out of the seat, feeling all the dark clouds lift. My stomach ache disappears, and I smile so hard it hurts. Happy tears rush to my eyes. I sniffle them back as I plaster myself to Blade in a bear hug. "I'm so happy," I say, fighting my wobbling chin. "You're going to make me cry."

His hands clasp my face tenderly, and I melt into his stare. "Don't you get it, Annalisa?" he whispers. "I can't say goodbye to you, darlin'. You said you could see me as your man. Well, this is me, being your man."

Warm tears tumble down my cheeks. I can't believe what I'm hearing. I wrap my arms around him and kiss every part of his handsome face. "Ahem." Timothy's voice brings me back to the here and now. The plane fires up, and the engine's roar fills the car.

"The pilot is on your schedule," Blade yells over the noise. "I can't have you late for your meeting." He smugly smiles. "Are you ready?"

I nod, barely able to contain my excitement. "Yes!"

He gives me a gentle kiss before Timothy helps me out of the car. Blade hurries around from his side and takes my hand.

We rush over the tarmac and take the stairs up to the plane. When I reach the top step, I stop. I can't resist looking down from this vantage point. I've flown a lot, but never this way. The sun makes the black asphalt sparkle, and I take in a breath. I guess there's a first time for everything.

"Does everything meet your approval?" Blade's eyes dart to me and then out to Timothy, who's still standing by the car, his back as straight as a soldier's.

"Yes. I just never want to forget this moment." I turn around and take that last step and enter the plane.

The first thing I smell is roses, and then that expensive leather scent that seems to follow Blade wherever he goes hits my nose.

"Welcome." A pretty flight attendant greets me holding a silver tray with two champagne flutes.

"Thank you," I say, taking the crystal glass, and peek behind me at Blade. "This is amazing." I overenunciate the words so he can hear me over the engine. He sends me a cocky grin in response.

The attendant pulls the curtain open behind her and ushers me through. I continue on to the cabin and almost drop my glass. I gawk with my mouth hanging open at the hundreds and hundreds of red roses covering almost every surface of the cabin. "Blade," I say under my breath, turning to see him enter through the curtain. I hear a metal door slam shut, and the plane goes quiet. "What's all this?"

He devilishly tips his champagne flute against mine. "Oh those?" He grins, gesturing to all the flowers with his glass. "Just your standard onboard flight entertainment. Welcome to Blade Airlines."

The cabin looks more like a living room than a plane. "Here," he says, leading me to a couch with seat belts. Thankfully, I sit down before my legs give out. I'm so overwhelmed I'm shaking and don't know where to look first.

"Thank you," I say softly. "This is all so incredibly beautiful." I notice the enormous flower arrangement behind him. "Is that going to fall over when we take off?" I don't want anything to hurt my cowboy.

He laughs. "Always analyzing. No, darlin', there's a special glue they use to keep everything in place.

"May I offer you anything else before we begin our departure?" the flight attendant asks, topping off our glasses.

"Um, no, thank you."

"Mr. Parker?"

"I'm fine for now," Blade says with a gleam in his eye, and I know something's up. This is technically a work day for me. I shouldn't even be drinking. I have no idea what's going on with all the red roses. The only thing I'm certain of is Valentine's Day doesn't come in June.

"Breakfast and your other order will be served as soon as the pilot gives us the okay," the attendant says to Blade before disappearing through the curtain.

The seatbelt sign flashes overhead, and Blade stays suspiciously quiet as we buckle up. We hold hands during takeoff. My heart races. I peek over at him and catch his eye under his hat. "What are you up to?" I arch my brow.

"Nothing. Nothing at all. I'm just here for the ride to California," he says, not convincing me one little bit.

"We didn't even have to go through security. No waiting in line. No bags to check." I sigh, snuggling against his broad chest. "This is the life."

He winks. "Get used to it, darlin'."

Breakfast comes on bone china plates served from sterling silver trays the moment the seat belt sign goes off. Now I'm beginning to realize the extent of the Parker wealth. Blade wasn't kidding when he welcomed me to Blade Airlines. When I ask him about the details of chartering a plane, he confessed he didn't have to book this one. He owns it and had it flown in from Texas last night.

Just as I settle in, the attendant comes back to deliver a mouthwatering plate of designer chocolates and— "Are those brownies?"

"Those are the brownies I made the other night." He waggles his brows. "Luckily, I managed to save a few for my favorite chocoholic before Cash ate them all."

"Well, that's it then." I sniff back tears. "Now I'm definitely going to cry."

"Don't cry, my little sugar whiskey." Blade reaches over and kisses me.

"They're happy tears," I say, wiping them away with my fingers, and then grab a napkin. "No one has ever been this nice to me," I confess, the floodgates opening. "No one has ever been more thoughtful."

He kisses my tears away.

"Blade," I burst out. I want to tell him exactly how I feel, but I don't want to scare him, and I don't know if it's right to say it so soon. "I lov—like, I l—"

"I'm in love with you, Annalisa," he says, taking the words out of my mouth. He gets out of his seat and down on one knee in front of me.

What is he doing?

Blade reaches into his jacket pocket and pulls out a red velvet box. "You can forget about the 'like' with me. I was going to wait until your meeting was over, but I can't. I'm so in love with you, Annalisa, I couldn't wait another minute to tell you." He opens the box and takes my trembling hand in his.

My heart collapses when I see the tears mist in my cowboy's eyes too. "You've wrapped my heart around your finger, and now, if you don't mind, I'm going to put this on yours." I stare in stunned silence as he takes the ring from the box. "Now, this is only a promise ring," he says, sliding the jeweled ring onto my left ring finger. And it's a perfect fit.

Flabbergasted, I gaze down at the enormous red stone surrounded by diamonds. "A ruby?" I ask breathlessly, moving my hand a fraction of an inch. Rainbow sparkles flash through the cabin.

"I thought red would be appropriate, since it's the color of the heart you own," he says, bringing his hand to his heart. Blade's crystal-blue eyes find mine. "As soon as your meeting is over, I want to fly you to Texas and visit our family jeweler so we can pick out your engagement ring together."

"Oh my God." I finally understand what all the roses were about and that this isn't a boyfriend-girlfriend promise ring. It's something far more permanent, and all my dreams are coming true. "Are you asking me to ... ?"

"I know it's soon, but I've been waiting my whole life to find you, and I don't want to spend another day without you. Will you marry me, Annalisa?"

"Yes." The word spills from my lips as the tears rush over my cheeks.

"My heart is yours, Annalisa."

"I was so worried about having to say goodbye to you," I say, laughing and crying and barely seeing his gorgeous face through my tears.

"We'll love each other and be man and wife forever." He kisses me as we soar into the clouds.

"And ever, my love, my one and only. My cowboy."

Epilogue

THREE MONTHS LATER

Blade proposed to me three months ago, and we made it official after I made him sign a prenup. I never want him to think that I love him for anything other than the perfect man he is. Joseph James didn't balk a bit about me leaving. He said he'd never get in the way of true love. He's here right now, sitting next to Vivian and my mother in the front row.

After our honeymoon, if I want to work, Blade says his family business will keep me more than busy.

The sun beams down on us like it's coming from heaven. Blade and I are standing in front of the largest, oldest oak tree in Texas. Garlands of white roses, gardenias and sweet jasmine wind and twist through the delicate limbs of the tree. Enormous chandeliers drip with crystals from the thick, larger branches above. Mrs. Parker says they'll look even prettier tonight at the reception when all the candles are lit.

I stare at my handsome groom, and then out to the rows of chairs festooned with flowers and smiling guests. The Parkers' stately three-story mansion stands behind them. Casa de Estrellas is dressed to the nines, with flowers and garlands on every balcony. Even her windows seem to be sparkling with joy.

Mrs. Parker wasn't kidding when she said "In Texas, we go big or go home." Everything about Casa de Estrellas is spectacularly overwhelming, yet homey and warm at the same time. This is the most elaborate wedding I've ever been to.

I can't believe I'm the bride.

Blade told me he wouldn't be nervous today, and my cowboy is true to his word. He's cool as a cucumber and more handsome than ever in his tuxedo and black dress Stetson. His blue eyes lock with mine, and my heart floats up to the clouds.

I gaze down at my sparkling ring and hold my breath as I slide my beautiful man's wedding ring onto his left finger. I stare up at him through happy tears and know in my heart that time doesn't matter, not when you're us. Not when your love is meant to be.

We say "I do" in a blur of happiness, and when the preacher says, "You may now kiss the bride," Blade takes me in his arms and dips me in one of those made-for-the-movies kisses.

The crowd erupts in cheers as he takes my hand in his and we run down the aisle. Under thousands of flower petals, we laugh, bursting with joy, racing together toward forever and ever.

"I'VE NEVER SEEN BLADE happier," Mom says, smiling, looking twenty years younger than she did last week. She, my sister, Scarlett, and my new sister-in-law, Annalisa, only had two and a half months to put this shindig together. Of course, they had the best wedding planner Parker money can buy to help them.

"That's one down." I chuckle and catch sight of my baby girl running on the lawn in her frilly pink dress. Her pretty bow is lopsided and her auburn ringlets dance around her shoulders. Mom follows my sightline and watches Maribelle with me. "She's been tearing around this place like a maniac," I comment, searching for Mrs. White, Belle's temporary nanny.

"It's all that sugar." Mom laughs. "She keeps sweet-talking everyone into giving her another piece of cake."

"Of course she does, and who can resist the most beautiful girl in the world?"

Belle jumps when she sees that I'm watching her. Her face lights up and she makes a beeline for me, running as fast as her little legs will carry her.

I bend, spreading my arms open wide. "Gotcha!" Belle giggles as I lift her and twirl her in a hug.

"Daddy?" She solemnly peers into my eyes, running a frosting-covered finger down my cheek. "Are we going to dance too?"

"I've saved all my dances for you, sweetheart." I kiss her nose as Mrs. White hurries toward us. I almost feel bad that I gave her the job. She mentioned she needed knee surgery, and she's wincing with every step she takes.

"Mr. Parker," she states professionally. "Ma'am," she greets my mother and turns to my daughter. "Shall we wash your hands, Belle, and tuck you in for a nap?"

"It's probably a good idea," I say, and Belle frowns. My mother went all out decorating a bedroom just for Belle to use whenever we visit. "It doesn't have to be a long nap, and I'll come in and wake you when it's time for our dance."

"Promise?" Belle rubs her little button nose against mine.

"Promise." She nods with a grin, and I carefully set her down to let Mrs. White take her back to the house.

Mom folds her arms and observes the two of them slowly walking up the gleaming marble staircase. "Have you had a chance to think about hiring Nicky as Belle's nanny?"

"Not yet. I haven't even seen her."

"Well, if you lived here, instead of in that cold top-floor penthouse in Dallas, you'd see her more often. I've been inviting her to the house any chance I get. She's been cooped up on her father's old ranch for too long."

I nod amiably, still not committed to the idea Mom brings up every time we talk. She's been trying to convince me to hire Billy Bowman's daughter as Belle's nanny. Even though Billy was ten years older, we were pretty close for a time. It crushed all of us when he died after his battalion ran over an IED in Afghanistan. "I haven't seen Nicolette since the funeral. The only thing I remember is the black dress she was wearing and the tears on her cheeks. What is she, twenty now?"

"Twenty-one, and you can't miss her." Mom zeros in on me. "She's the only one wearing a bikini at the pool."

I raise my brows.

"Houston, she has no one," Mom scolds, even though I haven't said a damn word. "I'm afraid she's going to get into all kinds of trouble. She needs a proper job. And you need a nanny. Why don't you give the poor girl a chance and hire her?" Mom asks, even though she's made it clear she won't be taking no for an answer. "That way, you and Belle can join us in Montana. We need you there."

I blow out a breath and sip my beer. She's right, of course. It's becoming more and more difficult to manage my end of our new Montana project while living in Texas. "I'll tell you what."

Mom's blue eyes brighten.

"I'll track her down and talk to her."

"Thank you, darlin.'" She reaches up on tiptoe and giddily kisses my cheek. "And if you don't make a final decision tonight, you can wrap up the details tomorrow. She's coming to the barbeque."

"Hey, I'm not making any promises, okay? Please don't get your hopes up." I can see the words fly right past her satisfied smile.

"I just know you two will hit it off. Belle already loves her. You should've seen them together at lunch last week." She tucks a stray hair into her bun. "I won't keep you," she says excitedly, giving my arm a squeeze. "You go ahead and find her while I check in with the wedding planner. I think it's almost time for Blade and Annalisa to leave for their honeymoon."

I sigh, watching her walk back through the crowd of adoring friends. If I'm going to talk to Nicolette today, I should get this over with now. I won't have a minute to myself when Belle wakes up from her nap. And I'm not complaining. Belle is the best part of my life, but being a single father is a lot of work. I wouldn't mind a little help.

I make my way around Casa de Estrellas to the pool area. There isn't much of a crowd, but I'm guessing most of the younger guests are hanging out here. Hey, there's a full bar—why not? I order another beer and scan the cabanas and then the lounge chairs by the pool's edge.

Goddamn.

I think that's her. My eyes fix on a sexy-as-fuck young thing coming out of the pool. I can't take my eyes off her long, lithe body as she bends over in the tiniest white thong bikini. The water from the pool beads over the best ass I've seen in my life. Her breasts are just the right size. I could take the whole of one in my mouth.

I lock on to her hard nipples and swallow. My cock swells, and I quickly turn away. I shouldn't stare. What is wrong with me? She's my friend's daughter, a good ten years younger than me, and off fucking limits.

I turn, checking her out again. She's young as sin. I can't stop imagining what it would be like to taste her sweet pussy and drill her little fuck-hole.

Christ. I've been so lonely.

No fucking way am I hiring her. It would be playing with fire. I wouldn't be able to keep my hands off her.

Then again, I haven't been fucked in two years, and I *do* need the help ...

STAY UP TO DATE WITH Adriana's latest releases by visiting her website:

www. AdrianaFrench.com

Made in United States
Troutdale, OR
12/04/2023